Will There Be Rapt

- Janet Frank's Enquiry

By Yemi Bankole

'Here is a true portrayal of the coming event...remarkably made plain in words that are concise and gripping...'

'A work that renders well its content...intellectually enticing.'

'A spiritual read...a tantalising mystery...a superb account of the City of Coveland drawn with an eschatological pencil.'

About the book - Prefatory Note

Will There Be Rapture and Any '666'? is a cluster of events that cruise along in series with regard to the current world order, and how they affect Africa, Great Britain, America and the Caribbean, including towns, homes and individuals up to Janet Frank, who mysteriously disappears with some people and leaves parents behind in the city of Coveland.

A well crafted plot, Janet Frank's odyssey answers many often asked questions like: Will the world truly end? Is there correlation between the end and the Rapture? What is Rapture? Is there reality in it? When and where will it take place? Who should experience the Rapture? And is Rapture the end of our world?

As world's epic narrative, the novel labours to take care of controversial themes as: the Marriage Supper, the 7-year Great Tribulation otherwise known as

Daniel's 70th Week, the man Antichrist or Beast, his personality, his mark and his government.

Answers are provided for such questions as: What is Great Tribulation? What is '666'? When is '666' to be introduced? Who will introduce it? What happens to those who collect this mark? How are those who reject it to be treated? These and many other thoughtful questions are dramatically unravelled in this intriguing, suspense-full, oven-hot novel, that remains fresh, warm, busy releasing 'steam' from the introduction to the conclusion.

Please, get seated, read and be informed.

About the Author

Yemi Bankole is a researcher and writer with soul-related articles for the youth and adult. He speaks in language forums and addresses Christian gatherings on basic issues of life. Yemi lives in Nigeria and works in the CCED of Olabisi Onabanjo University, Nigeria. He can be reached on oluyemibankole68@gmail.com, Whatsapp: 08130699308; hotline: +234-8029550501 a text Message is preferred.

Please, kindly send this book to a friend, family and neighbour. Thank you.

About Otakada.org

At God's Eagle Ministries Otakada.org, We are seeding the Nations with Over 2 Million Christian Centric Content, and God is Transforming Lives Through the Timeless Truth in His Word!

Together with YOU, we are building MASSIVE SPIRITUAL TEMPLES in OUR HEARTS for the Spirit of God to DWELL in and OPERATE through with EASE in these TIMES and SEASONS, so STAY with us and BUILD with us as God Heals, Delivers, and Restores our Souls In Jesus Name, Amen!

Check this out in *1 Thessalonians 5:23, 2 Timothy 1:7 Hebrews 4:12-13; 1 Corinthians 3: 1- 17; Leviticus 26:12; Jeremiah 32:38; Ezekiel 37:27; 2 Corinthians 6:16; 1 John 4:4*

Read – 1 Thessalonians 5:23 Amplified Bible (AMP) [23] *Now may the God of peace Himself sanctify you through and through [that is, separate you from profane and vulgar things, make you pure and whole and undamaged— consecrated to Him—set apart for His purpose]; and may your spirit and soul and body be kept complete and [be found] blameless at the coming of our Lord Jesus Christ.*

Our Mission at God's Eagle Ministries ties in with Ephesians 4:1-16, to seek out the best of the best five (5) fold ministry gifts in the body of Christ, so that they can equip the saints for the work of Ministry (Laborers are few indeed, whilst there are ripe harvest of souls all around us waiting to be harvested) equipping continues till we all come to the unity of faith as loudly proclaimed in the place of prayer by Jesus Himself in John 17.

Our core passion is to point the saints, who are sons of our Father God to Christ, who is the head of the body according to the order of

John 1:12-13

Amplified Bible, Classic Edition

12 But to as many as did receive and welcome Him, He gave the authority (power, privilege, right) to become the children of God, that is, to those who believe in (adhere to, trust in, and rely on) His name—

13 Who owe their birth neither to bloods nor to the will of the flesh [that of physical impulse] nor to the will of man [that of a natural father], but to God. [They are born of God!]

and Ephesians 1:5

He predestined us to adoption as sons through Jesus Christ to Himself, according to the kind intention of His will

But not as jobless sons but those who are well equipped through core practical oriented Discipleship so that they can launch out as a mighty army to go make disciples of all nations without regards to denomination for we are one in Christ Jesus, amen.

To promote Christ in us – sons of a mighty God, the hope of glory!

Colossians 1:26-27 "The Mystery of the kingdom is simply this: Christ in you! Yes, Christ in you bringing with him the hope of all glorious things to come. '" It goes on to say that "the hope of glory is the fulfillment of God's promise to restore us and all creation" – Hallelujah!

To break it down further, Our Passion *at God's Eagle Ministries – Otakada.org and the body of Christ, in general, is to equip faith-based communities and to reach online seekers through wholesome content, products, and services that enhance holistically the spirit, the soul, and the body of the individual and to foster unity in the body of Christ!*

We are passionately passionate to intercede, to see, to experience and to deploy by the help of His Holy Spirit, UNITY of SPIRIT in and amongst the saints of God in Christ Jesus according to Jesus prayer in John 17 – That we will be one in Christ Jesus.

Who We are at God's Eagle Ministries, Otakada.org is tied to our *values, vision, and mission* as highlighted hereunder:

Our Values: Integrity, Excellence, Speed, and profitability.

Our Vision: We envision a discipled world.

Our Mission: All our resources will be geared towards creating and distributing engaging Christian content for the discipling of all nations

Our goal at God's Eagle Ministries Otakada.org is to effectively engage *100 million souls by 2040 as the Lord tarries*...stay with us.

You can partner with what we do by visiting our partnership page https://www.otakada.org/partnership-giving/

visit https://shop.otakada.org for ebooks and paperback to help you grow in the lord

Table of Contents

PART ONE

1- The MORNING of vacation

It was 6, o'clock in the female hostel of Saint Beckley Grammar School early one Thursday morning, being the closing day of the first term, when Bukky, a senior student, woke up from her sleep. She sat up; wore an entirely mournful face, the reflection of a mind battling with a confusing thought. Before long, drops of tears had begun to ooze from her eyes in succession with sweat clustering fast on her forehead. Around that time, a junior student named Janet, whose bed was next to Bukky's, awoke too. Surprised to see Senior Bukky in tears, Janet, with concern, jumped out of her bed and moved close to her. Of course, Bukky had been an approachable student who loved to take care of others and teach them Mathematics, especially the junior ones in her hostel. Little wonder, those junior students liked to call her Senior 'B' for short.

"Good morning Senior Bukky," Janet greeted.

"Janet, how are you?"

"Fine."

Sitting beside Bukky, Janet asked, "Senior B, hope there is nothing wrong? Your mood is somehow this morning."

"It's true Janet. I had a dream overnight. What I saw has kept worrying me since I woke up." With her nightgown, Bukky mopped her face of tears once and again.

"Senior B, dream? Dream is nothing to worry about. You see, whenever I have a bad dream, I'll just ignore it; since whenever I have a good one it doesn't come to pass. Why then worrying myself...."

"Janet, it's true. But this is an unusual dream."

"Uh-huh...! Well," Janet concurred.

"You see, in my dream, Jesus the Son of God appeared to take away his saints. In the dream, I saw that I was taking a walk on our street at home one evening, and it was busy drizzling. All of a sudden, the sky turned yellow like the evening sunray. There appeared in the sky an indescribable gate that looked like the entrance into the Celestial City talked about in the Bible. Within a split second, something like an elevator began to carry me toward the entrance. I was going and going with my two arms lifted. The movement was supernatural and fast. It remained just a little moment for me to pass through the gate into the great beyond, when I opened my eyes, only to discover that I was back in my bed in the hostel."

Janet's mouth fell open in astonishment. "How beautiful for me to have gone just like that...," Bukky anticipated.

"I have never had such a dream; though I have heard people say they dreamt of something like that. Anyway, Senior B, this issue of end time, how true is it? Will there be Rapture or any '666'?"

"Janet, is like you too don't believe that Rapture is real?"

"Not so, but then I have once heard the Physics Master tell David and Sandra that there was nothing like Rapture. He said that Rapture was both a religious dogma and mental of a thing."

"Our Physics teacher, are you sure?"

"Yes of course!"

Shocked, Bukky immediately brought out her Bible.

"Janet…"

"Ma."

"Comparing the Physics Master with God, who's greater?"

"God is."

"Besides, who made the heaven?" she pointed to the sky.

"God, Senior B."

"Okay. What of the earth, was it our Physics Master?"

"No! It was God!"

"So, let me now show you the utterance of that God whose words are valid forever. Let's read from the Bible in First Thessalonians Chapter 4 verses 13-14."

She opened her Bible and began to read while Janet kept listening.

> 'But I would not have you to be ignorant, brethren, concerning them which are asleep, that ye sorrow not, even as others which have no hope. For if we believe that Jesus died and rose again, even so them also which sleep in Jesus will God bring with him. For this we say unto you by the word of the Lord, that we which are alive and remain unto the coming of the Lord shall not prevent those which are asleep,'

I hope you're following..." Bukky paused and enquired.

"Yes, I am."

"Now, we are in verse sixteen, '*For the Lord Himself shall descend from heaven with a shout, with the voice of the archangel, and with the trump of God: and the dead in Christ shall rise first. Then we which are alive and remain shall be caught up together with them in the clouds, to meet the Lord in the air; and so shall we ever be with the Lord.*'

"Janet, you see when Jesus comes at this time, He'll not reveal Himself to the whole world. Rather, He'll stay in the sky with his angels who will blow the trumpets. When the trumpets sound, all the dead but converted souls will resurrect in a glorious body to meet the Lord Jesus in the sky. Then those Christians who're on earth and have not died would be changed and off they'd go to meet the Lord. This event is as true as God is, and can happen any moment from now. We're encouraged never to be ignorant of it. If anybody argues against it, it only shows that such a one is ignorant of the truth. His argument in the contrary does not invalidate this eternal truth."

Troubled, Janet asked.

"Senior Bukky, please are you sure I'd go when it happens?"

"Janet, ah! Nobody can assure you of that. You have to be sure of it yourself..."

"Senior B, don't let me deceive you, it doesn't appear such assurance is in me!"

"But you can have it Janet, if only you do what the scripture demands from anyone who wishes to be *raptured*."

"What and what do the scripture demand?"

"The first is this. You must acknowledge your sin..."

"Sin?"

"Yes, sin. Sin is any crime that is committed against God's written Commandments or any other done contrary to His holy way as engraved within our consciences. The following are examples: anger, fighting, lying, cursing, cheating in the exam, exposing one's privates by wearing indecent dresses, keeping of a boyfriend as a girl, fornication, masturbation, gay or homosexuality, and so on and so forth. The next step you take is that you sincerely confess all your sins to God from your heart, asking for forgiveness on the merit of Christ's death on the tree. Next to this is that you accept Jesus as your Saviour and Lord."

"But Senior B, are you sure all you've just mentioned are really sinful, after all majority of people do them even those we call Christians? In fact, many ministers' wives and lady evangelists often showcase sensitive parts of their bodies too like Hollywood actresses. I've seen 'Christian teachers', even among those that preach in this school chapel, giving answers to their favourite students in the exam hall. So, what are we talking about?"

"Janet, hun-n-n, let me ask you. How many people perished in the flood at Noah's time?"

"Uncountable."

"How many were saved?"

"Just eight."

"Who and who?"

"Noah, his children and their wives."

"This is what happened. Other people sinned except Noah! And when they perished, they perished except Noah! God is not bothered by any church title. What he demands from every man is genuine repentance. Unless one repents, one may still perish even with one's religious title. Religious office will be useless in the day of reckoning and Christians by mouth profession but sinful by lifestyle will be disappointed in the end."

"What about someone like me who has been accepting Jesus all these days in the church, at home and even on the assembly ground during the morning devotions?"

"Janet, let me tell you, a new life of salvation experience does not come that way. If your decision is not precise and confession total, you would only have casual repentance and really nothing would change in you. It has to be clear to you that becoming a child of God is not tied to the number of confessions you make but to the sincerity of your confession and readiness to break with sin and walk with God. It is on the proviso that one stands on one's decision not to sin again that heaven retains one's name in the Book of Life. It is only such a person that will go up to meet the Bridegroom at His return."

Janet, on hearing these, laid herself bare to conviction and out of guilt enquired:

"Senior Bukky, I'm still a sinner. If I say it is well with my soul on this issue of conversion, I will only be fooling myself. But does God truly forgive?"

"Yes, He does if we satisfy the condition.

Senior Bukky passionately explained further what it takes to be saved from sin until the latter grabbed it all and replied:

"I am ready."

At this time, Janet had already knelt down beside the bed and Bukky, still by her, led her in prayer when she said this:

"Janet, as we pray now, make a choice. Be open to God by confessing all your sins to Him. You should ask for his mercy. Call on Jesus to come into your heart. Promise God that you will no more go back to those sins..."

Janet and Bukky prayed that morning. The former became so free at heart for the guilt that was removed and the peace of God that overflowed her soul. It was just a few minutes after 6.o'clock that morning

2 - ♫ GOOD-bye teachers...

GOOD-bye friends ♫

In the noon of that Thursday, the school closed for the term. Joy filled Bukky and Janet because they had both done well in their first term examination. However, Janet seemed not to be as much excited by her result as by her new life in Christ and the assurance that she could hear the trumpets of the angels any moment from then.

Because it was a time for boarders to go back home after months of staying away from their loved ones, many parents came in their cars to pick their wards. Some parents sent their drivers while few students had to travel home by themselves. On the said day, the whole school premises wore a new look with the parade of flashy cars everywhere. Janet and Bukky also had to go home. They had packed their things and were busy discussing that morning prayer, as they moved out of the school premises to the main gate to board vehicles.

"Senior Bukky, please keep on praying for me. Now I know within me that I'm truly of God. I've now discovered that keeping sin partners commonly called boyfriends and dressing in clothes that leave out girls' sensitive parts of the body are devil's devices to keep female students in bondage. Since we prayed in the morning, I have developed deep hatred for those sinful relationship and habits that had made themselves lords over my soul."

"No cause for alarm, Janet. God will keep you. Your present experience is an index of a genuine conversion," Bukky responded happily.

"Senior B, you know Thompson K. now..."
"Thompson K., do I? Em...," trying to recall.
"You should know him; he's the son of the PTA Chairman..."

"Okay! Okay! Yes, Thompson... I know the boy. He's in the Arts Class."

"Yes. He used to be my boyfriend. To let you know how close we were, he had given me the transport fare for this journey. His home address was with me and I had arranged to pay him a visit during the vac. But after the prayer you had with me in the morning, I couldn't cope with all I had collected from him. So, I returned his money, the wrist-watch he bought for me and his home address to him."

"Is that true?"

"Yes. Just there at the assembly hall after the Principal's farewell address, I went to him and returned everything. I told him what had happened to me and that I wouldn't be able to cope with heaven if he remained in my life. I let him realize that such sinful relationship would prevent me from facing my academics and pleasing my Lord."

"Fine! That's a mark of a true Christian life. But what did he say?"

"Well, he was angry and would like to know who told me all that. I just left his sight immediately."

"Thank God for that, that's the best approach to it, lest he wins your heart again with sweet words."

While their journey to the main gate continued, Bukky and Janet held each other's hands. Their discussion extended to what they intended doing during the four-week holiday, especially how they would help their parents. They reminded each other of the resumption date, when they would meet again in the hostel. They also exchanged their parents' telephone numbers to facilitate communication during the vacation.

"Now Janet," Bukky continued, "...we're parting very soon, greet Dad and Mum and everybody at home.

Don't forget your Bible and prayer. Pray very well and read your books also."

"Alright."

"Have this token for your transport," Bukky offered a peanuts.

"Oh no! Senior Bukky, don't worry to give me anything. I've decided to trek home."

"Never! I'll rather trek than for you to."

Smiling, Bukky held Janet and tried to shovel the transport fare into her pocket.

"No, no...," Janet objected.

"Don't reject the chicken feed. Don't be shy. Take the money and go to the car park immediately," Bukky insisted.

"Thank you Senior Bukky," she eventually collected the money.

"Don't mention. God bless you."

"B-y-e, Senior B."

"Bye! Bye! Janet."

Senior Bukky dismissed Janet Frank with a wave.

They parted just like that, not knowing it was for life.

3 - BORN again or BORN against?

Holiday is a time of rest and less of brain gymnastics. More food is taken and more visits to friends and uncles are paid. Because of all it involves, many students do wish that holiday does not end. They have forgotten that if wishes were horses, beggars might ride.

Before anybody knew it, the holiday had long gone. Like a dream, Janet had spent about three weeks at home with her family. Mr. and Mrs. Frank, her parents, were influential people. They lived in their own house along the popular Oak Street in Coveland. They had a new model of Japanese car with San Hassan as their driver.

As part of Janet's resolve to help her parents during the ongoing break, she was about to go for shopping for her mum one afternoon.

"Jan-e-t," Mrs. Frank called.

"Y-e–s mummy," she ran inside from the backyard.

"Go and dress up. You're going with the driver to buy some things for me from the market."

"Yes Ma."

Janet went in and, in few minutes later, returned to the sitting room.

"Why? Skirt and blouse to market? Don't you know what girls of your age wear today? Put on one of your trousers and jersey." Mrs. Frank firmly ordered.

"Ah, Mum, do I have to?"

"Why?"

"I wouldn't like to wear such a dress again, especially trousers."

"I said why?"

"It's indecent for a female Christian," Janet innocently affirmed.

Intently looking at her, Mrs. Frank asked,

"Where are your earrings by the way? Or…"

"Mummy, so you never noticed that since I came…" Janet cut in on her mum.

"That what?" Mrs. Frank asked, gawking at her in anger.

"That I didn't bring them back from school."

"Why?"

"I threw them away when I read Isaiah 3 verses 16-21 right inside the cab when coming home from school."

"Something is wrong with your head. Trousers are not good; earrings too are bad, eh? (Clapped hands). Who preached to you?" Turned to Mr. Frank, "Daddy, look at your Jane…," pointing to her in anger.

"It's good you noticed it yourself. Because I've been wondering since her arrival from hostel of what has become of her. Don't you observe how she prays at the family altar? Besides, she now does things like the *home-*

goer in the next street who doesn't know more than 'born again' and 'holy life'..., replied Mr. Frank.

Home-goer was the nickname given to any member of *Christ Home-going Church* at Oak Community. The church in question, though had a few members, was renowned for thorough teaching of the Bible truth in Coveland Metropolis.

"Don't worry, time will tell whether you're born again or born against. I give you a week. You will soon discover that *beans is not fit for supper*. Foolish! Go! Go! Go out of my sight. When you come back, you'll explain yourself!" Mrs. Frank dismissed Janet.

She was heading for the door when Frank himself called her back.

"Janet, don't go yet. Come. You'll buy me a bottle of Sunshine Beer from the market," he brought out money from his pocket.

Turned back though, Janet suddenly developed heavy feet and heart, as she moved to her father. "Ah! Sunshine Beer, Daddy? Why not go for some soft drink?"

"What's it? Or at thirteen you don't know the popular Sunshine Larger Beer?" Frank bellowed.

"Daddy, I do...but...but...," stammered, "...it's not good for your health and, as a Christian, taking and giving of alcohol is a sin before our God. As my father, buying you such a thing places a question mark on my relationship with God. In fact, it is like giving you a poison and God forbid," Janet declared, pleading on her knees, shaking slightly for nervousness with her arms up like those of praying mantis,.

"You better bottle up your dirty mouth there. Nasty parrot! You better go and run commentary for a radio station. Wait, that Principal of yours is he a *Home-goer*? Mrs. Frank harshly confronted Janet.

"No mummy!"

"No? Okay, we're going to see him to know who stuffed your head with all this madness. Rubbish, *Sunshine* is a poison, *shmm...*," berserk, Mrs. Frank hissed.

"Get up and go to the market for your mummy. I have no case with you but with your hostel mistress. It is for education I sent you to Beckley College and not for all this rubbish."

Janet went out dispirited, having been thoroughly wounded at heart with shots of questions like bullets.

4- MARRIAGE of 'bed first' BEFORE the altar of 'I do'

In the City of Coveland, Dave Pauli lived at 5, Justice Street. Dave was in his late twenties, an account officer in an oil firm. Dave's wedding with Florence was a few weeks ahead. For this reason, he was on leave and Florence, his wife to-be, was on visit to him. Florence pressed the ring.

"Who you?"

"Me."

"Come in," Dave ordered.

"How, Flore?" Dave asked curiously.

"Uh...," Florence sighed in dejection as she took her seat.

"Were you at Royal Road Hospital for the test?"

"I'm just from there; we're in trouble Dave..."

"What is it?" Dave asked in anxiety.

"I'm pregnant."

"Pregnant? How? No, that can't be!" tapping his fingers. "Wedding is three Saturdays away."

"We gave the devil a metre; he went a mile," Florence regretted aloud.

After much weeping, Dave enquired, "What did they say?"

"Well, the doctor in charge, seeing my sad countenance after the test, asked for any problem whatever. I told him that we were getting wedded three weeks' time and that the preparation was at the peak. But that our church wouldn't conduct the wedding if it was detected that I was pregnant."

"Hope you didn't mention the church in question?"

"No! Eventually he said that the only solution was to go for abortion."

"Florence, we, abortion?" Dave interrupted.

"I don't k–n–o–w!" she too became confused.

"Hun... abortion is delicate. Anyway, how safe are you?" Dave inquired.

"He showed me the list of the people, about five or so, who had done it just before I got there this morning."

"Abortion, h–a–a, anyway, if that is the only way out," Dave replied.

"But one of the matrons, who, I guess, is a *home-goer* because of the way she dressed and talked, heard the discussion and later called me when I came out of the doctor's office. She asked whether I am a Christian. I told her I am, though I didn't tell her that I'm preparing for any wedding. She told me never to go for abortion whatever had happened. That, besides its inherent danger, all who committed abortion wouldn't see God but suffer in hell. In fact, she told me to read Hebrews 9: 27-28."

"Well, we know that of course, but what do we do in this peculiar condition? I know the Matron. She's Mrs. Abdullah. She's a staunch member of Christ Home-going Church. She lives down the estate. Her husband has a house there."

"Dave, tell me what do we do?"

"It has happened. There is no other way than to terminate the issue. If we dare confess to the church and the wedding is interrupted or cancelled, the shame would be too much for us to bear. In the first place, what do we tell the dignitaries already invited for the occasion? Remember our chairman is a VIP. What do we even tell our parents, guests and friends? It's better you go for it tomorrow."

"Abortion?" Florence asked herself, her conscience being in grief.

"Florence, be brave, don't be a coward. Cowards die before their days."

"Dave it's not a matter of being a coward. I am thinking about heaven."

"Anyway, we shall settle that in prayer later. Please come tomorrow morning for the money," Florence sorrowfully consented and went away.

Florence went out not knowing she had signed her doom. About what led to their tragic fall into sexual mess, we have no sufficient information. But we heard from his neighbours that Dave would never do anything without consulting a close friend of his. According to them, most of Dave's actions were dictated by his friend. Even the counsel that Florence should be put in a family way before wedding was a supposed idea of the friend. That if Florence was not pregnant before their wedding, it was an index that she was not Dave's true 'bone'. They further disclosed that the friend himself when getting married went to the altar to be joined to a lady with a six-month-old pregnancy because of the fear of delay in child-bearing. Thus, it follows that he must have expressed the same fear to Dave and counselled him to follow suit.

Anyway, whether this information was true or otherwise of Dave's friend, no real evidence was in place. Notwithstanding, the scenario has demonstrated itself enough that Dave and Florence had violated the creed of holy wedlock ever before contracting it.

5- Coveland City GOSPEL centre

Coveland was typical of the present-day cities of the world in many respects. It was a model of every country, however modern, however remote. It wore the sophistication of mega city and exalted civilisation of the day to their utmost praises and brutish abuses. Like if you attempt to visit her markets for instance, you wouldn't have gone far before the odour of things produced in their factories begins to greet your nostrils. And your eyes will soon be weary of seeing automobiles you've never met in your country just by standing beside her roads. Within few minutes, as beautiful and exotic cars speed off with the sizzling sound of their engines and their glamour seizes your attention, you will see a long truck which rattles along and engages its driver in a battle with the steering wheel, as the man struggles to keep the old rickety auto on track. Hardly would you have settled properly well enough on a wonder, before another one emerges to greet your eyes. That is Coveland for you. In Coveland, there were several government reserved areas (GRAs). There were big commercial centres. Streets were being swept by road machines and street light never blinked for power failure. While security was on solid terrain in Coveland, mobile phones were every-hand friendly and internet was far from being a Western miracle. As public schools littered the city, being an effort of the government of the day to eradicate illiteracy, highbrow private institutions also existed for the first class citizens. New generation banks had found Coveland as a rich outlet for expansion, with their characteristic under-thirty young chaps in corporate outfits as staff members. Flashy cars with the ego that goes with them often sped on the asphalt-plated roads of Coveland in the night as in the day.

However, several places in Coveland were not better than what qualifies for ghettos, where the poor, ragamuffin and beggars erected their shanks. There were miscreants in Coveland, the type of 'area' boys found in some densely populated cities today, who consciously disturb the peace of the masses. Coveland had a strong religious base, only that it did not endorse a state religion. It is convenient therefore to say that hers was a secular state, where all religions co-existed without itch.

Talking about church, there were several of them in Coveland. Was it Orthodox? Their stone-structure cathedrals were all over the city. Was it Evangelical? Almost each street had its own. Pentecostals were uncountable. But truth was scarce! The few that stood on the Bible truth remained unpopular. Only music, gorgeous donations, dancing, and litany of empty services conducted in well polished English were the hallmarks of a whole lot of Pastor Mrs. and G.Os in this big city. Regrettably, many acclaimed dynamic churches in the land were hooked up in the end-time wave of investing people's offerings on building institutions, instead of fulfilling the law: *'that there may be meat in my house'.* Surprisingly, the said institutions were affordable to only the children of the political chieftains, senators, corrupt custom officers and godless business tycoons who used religion to cover up, and not to the children of their church members who carried their cross come rain, come sunshine and undertook less of worldly-enticing jobs to prevent being entangled by the lure and stains of riches. Sadly, these indigent Christians were often promised a reward in heaven by these leaders who rode jeeps and jets bought with the money of the poor tithe payers.

Very close to the time in question, a new church arose in Coveland: 'Daily Showers Interdenominational' by name, a.k.a *Coveland City Gospel Centre*. Daily Showers took off barely a year ago with Ray Fred as the Minister-in-charge. At the time of this story, its membership was in the vicinity of four hundred and fifty.

At quarter to seven one evening, praise worship had just ended at *Coveland City Gospel Centre* when Mr. Davidson and Mrs. Abdullah from Christ Home-going Church got to the location. They were on visit to Ray Fred's Church. Ray Fred, when at Home-going, used to be a member of the evangelism team of which his visitors were members till date. After few minutes of waiting, Ray's visitors were allowed in.

"Good evening Sir, and welcome Madam," Ray greeted Davidson and Abdullah.

"How are you?" replied Mr. Davidson.

"How are things my brother?" asked Mrs. Abdullah.

"Fine. Thank you. An usher just informed me about you now."

"We came in at the closing prayer of the service," disclosed Mr. Davidson.

"Is that so? That's great. You're welcome Sir."

Immediately, Ray Fred took his visitors to the church guests' room, where they had some chats and a discussion ensued.

"How do I entertain you tonight Sir? It's dark somehow, and eatery is far to this place. Or what do I do…Ehh?" hesitated Ray.

"Don't worry, we'll soon be going. You know Elder Davidson was away to Georgia on course when you left for this place. When he came two weeks ago while discussing with me, we made mention of you and I told him about your calling and new ministry. So he said we should visit you together," explained Mrs. Abdullah.

"It's a pleasure. That's nice of you. May heaven remember you too," reacted Ray.

"How is the ministry fairing?" asked Elder Davidson.

"Good. We are moving forward in the eagle's wings," hollered Ray Fred.

"I like that. It's good having the young people in the Lord's service. I thank the Lord for you. My counsel always to young ministers is that ministerial success is not tied to the number of the people one is able to gather together but to the volume of truth a minister is able to pass across to the people."

"Sure!" Ray admitted.

"As a minister of a young ministry, you must be sure of who and who share the altar with you, so that your purpose of being here will not be an empty dream..."

"I know all that already and God will keep his fold. Anyway, we are trying to be different here as the emphasis is shifting from what it used to be in the past. Daily Showers Interdenominational has received a mandate to address the gospel to the high profile class of our society. This, of course, calls for some modification in our approach to things... "

"But either high or low, I don't think the gospel has double standards," interrupted Elder Davidson.

"But Sir, you've seen things for yourself here. It's not an exaggeration! We started just some nine months ago, but today we are nearly five hundred. What do you expect two, three years ahead?

"This is because, here, the gospel is not scary, nor hard; rather, it is simple in nature, all-embracing and all-accommodating."

"But the road to heaven is narrow still, and Jesus said that few were those that found it," reacted the Elder.

"There you are? These are days of full gospel for all men. These are not days of hard sermons. Do you agree with me? That philosophy no longer works."

Ray got up as his voice gained volume. "The gospel audience of today are enlightened; therefore, we shouldn't shoot too many 'arrows' at them."

"Brother Ray, let Elder Davidson finish speaking…," interrupted Mrs. Abdullah.

"Oh! No! I'm saying the stage has shifted. People need liberation. Today's gospel is for liberation, success and liberty…"

"Ray, listen. What I'm saying is that you should always go back to the drawing board – the Bible – in all matters. The Bible is the final authority. It's dangerous to be an island to oneself," counselled Elder Davidson.

"We don't only prophesy here, we teach the Bible and preach the word too. Only that we don't put anybody in any confinement. And I said that without fear of contradiction."

"Ray, it's okay. You know, the servant of the Lord doesn't strive," declared Davidson.

"Yes, of course, of course," calming down.

"So, let's close the chapter and be praying for one another since we're all doing the Master's command," submitted Elder Davidson.

"Uh-huh…, good," Ray smiled. "That is what I expected you to say…"

"Brother Ray, try to understand us. We are not judging you neither are we trying to police you with regard to what you preach. Just as you know, all the Elder is saying is that as a young minister, you need to lay a solid foundation right at the outset and hold on to it."

"Thank you Matron, I do understand," appreciated Ray.

"Take care," responded Mrs. Abdullah.

"Let's have a word of prayer," demanded Elder Davidson.

Mrs. Abdullah rounded off the discussion with some prayer points touching the contents of their discussion. She solicited help from God on behalf of Pastor Ray Fred and his young ministry: Daily Showers Interdenominational.

6 - Courage of CONVICTION

As a sequel to being a cosmopolitan city, Coveland had reared many academic institutions and Coveland University, among others, could not be looked down upon. As an age-old institution, her dormitories were formidable edifices and her Senate building a stately structure, gazing serenely within the confinement of acres of well-trimmed pine trees. As she had witnessed several matriculation and graduation ceremonies, likewise had she weathered the storms of many union strikes and students' protests. However, no trace of dilapidation settled on her standard.

Coveland University insisted on merit. This was her scoring parameter. No '*godfathers*' when it comes to discipline. No 'long legs' to admission. The government of the day was not careful, as to be stingy, in the way she spent prodigally to sustain the institution's intellectual standard. As a result, Coveland University had never suffered any brain drain. Her seasoned educators were retained in their jobs.

Barely two weeks to the Rapture of the Church, specifically at 10.0' clock one Friday morning, Eze John, an undergraduate in the Faculty of Education, who was among those later raptured, headed for Professor Patrick's Office. The Prof. had told Eze to come around for some briefing on the last lecture he missed when the former sent him on errand. Eze, who was the class rep. of his department, entered the don's office at the time he was busy flipping through a postgraduate thesis on his table.

"Good morning Sir."

"Eze, how are you?"

With smile, "Fine, thank you Sir," Eze replied.

"For the briefing?" asked the Prof.

"Yes Sir."

"Have your seat, but give me some minutes."

Eze sat down and brought out his jotter as the Professor set at the business right away.

"Em... the lecture I taught the day I sent you to my publishers was 'The Tested Principles of High Performance for Classroom Learners'. Let me just have words with you. Now, just as educational planners ensure that educational policy favours a learner's overall needs, every competent teacher likewise must ensure his teaching benefits all categories of students under his instruction. More often than not, three major categories or groups of learners are identifiable in the four walls of the classroom. First, the poor; second, the average and third, the brilliant. Can you get me clearly, Eze?"

"Exactly Sir."

"Okay. Now, there is a principle basically designed for the poor to shift to the performing group of students. Here is the acronym for the principle: *RPIP+3D's* is equal to **VEP**." He repeated the formula again. "Have you put it down?" demanded Prof. Patrick.

"Yes... I'm doing that," Eze wrote down the formula.

The Prof. continued, "...now, the first component there, that is, **RPIP** means **Right Perspective of Inherent Potential**. The second component called **3D's** is **determination, discipline and diligence**. The result of these two components is **VEP**, which stands for **Visible Excellent Performance.** Is that clear?"

"Just some explanation Sir!"

"Get it clear, students whose average scores are between 1 and 49% fall into the category of the poor learners. To solve the problem of poor performance, the first thing is for the concerned student to develop a mindset that he has some untapped potential for high performance. He must sideline all inferiority complex or poor concept of self. Having done that, he must be determined to succeed not giving attention to all obstacles confronting his set-goals. After this, discipline follows. This is expressed in self-denial in eating habit, sleeping habit and time management. He must diligently study his books, burning mid-night candles...understood?"

"Yes Sir."

"Before he knows it, the result is sudden flight from the poor level to the success ladder – The **Visible Excellent Performance**: That's all..."

"Thanks Sir."

"Principle two, quick! I have to be fast a little bit. Principle two is for learners within the range of 50 and 59%. The formula is **SED** plus **BE = IPA**

Eze wrote it down.

"The meaning Sir?" he demanded.

"The three components mentioned in this principle are respectively: **Self Esteem Development** plus

Broadening Exercise = Increased Performance Ability.
Gotten?"

"Yes."

"What we're saying here is that mediocre students, who are neither poor nor also the best in their subjects, should come to realize that they are no less endowed. They should not write off themselves nor stake their problem of average performance for heredity. Self confidence or developed esteem must be put in place - a belief that I can do better. If the wrong concept must be dropped, such learners have to be told that mediocrity is not a matter of fate, luck or destiny. After this, they should foster some practical exercises towards self-development. That is, such student should visit the library; join discussion group or tutorial classes. The outcome of this is *Increased Performance Ability, IPA*."

"It's understood. Sir, should we postpone the rest to a later time, you're sweating already..."

"No! No! Just the last group is left."

"Okay Sir."

"Principle three right! The formula is **Dfsk + Ai = Om.**

This last principle is designed to keep the brilliant on the top rung of success ladder.

"That's okay Sir," Eze concurred, nodding his head for an assertive yes.

"The interpretation of **Dfsk + Ai = Om** is: **Discovery of new Fact, Sharing of Knowledge + Application of Idea = Optimum Maintenance.**"

"It's written," Eze said, raising his gaze.

"I'll explain in one word, while you read up the rest in your handout."

"Yes Sir."

"For a brilliant student who gathers his scores from 70 and above to maintain the status quo, one, he must be busy discovering new fact in his course of choice via journals, magazines and updated texts. Two, the knowledge newly gained should be shared with others for possible registering. He should apply the new idea to real life situation. The idea, of course, becomes an authentic theory after it has been applied and has been able to solve problems at hand. That's all, Eze."

"Thanks so much Sir."

"That's alright."

"When do you have my course next week?"

Eze checked his timetable.

"Monday Sir, but there is an Easter public holiday," he disclosed.

"Okay, Okay. These fanatics are at it again. Okay!"

On hearing this, Eze's countenance became dull, although he didn't utter a word.

"Or are you one of them?"

"Well, really Easter just reminds us of the death of the Saviour of mankind."

"So Jesus died for you," Prof. Patrick asked teasingly.

"He died for all sinners. In as much as I was a sinner, he died for me too."

"So, you're no more a sinner or what do you mean?"

"Sir, He has forgiven me when I repented."

"So all of us who have not repented are candidates for hell?"

"Sir, with all humility, God is no respecter of anyone. However, He has drawn a programme of Salvation for both the white and the black, even for the yellow in the North-East of Asia."

"Eze, thanks that you haven't forgotten your Geography. What I'm saying is not, however, Geography. I said how are you sure that you're forgiven?"

"I'm sure. I have the evidence. When a sinner confesses his sins to God with irrevocable determination not to go back to them, and he receives Jesus Christ, his sins are forgiven him. It is around this premise my evidence lies."

"How valid is this premise…Eze? I mean…," busy squeezing face to express utter disbelief.

"Sir, I am not just saying what I believe without a proof or what I rely upon without a ground for the claim. It is the scripture that says it and I take the same as final."

"Now, how far is it true that everybody is a sinner? Again, how possible is it for hell you people are talking about to accommodate the whooping number of sinners world over?"

"Sir, that everybody is a sinner is plain. If it is possible for all human beings to share the common anatomical features like the head, the legs and the hands in the process of conception, nothing makes it impossible for the hereditary nature of sin also to find an access into our being right at the womb. This is how exactly the sinful nature has passed on to all races of humanity without discrimination. Therefore, every typical human being, white, black or yellow, is a potential sinner irrespective of status and belief, until conversion to a new life through Jesus takes place. Confirming this, the Bible says, *'For all have sinned and come short of the glory of God.'* As for hell, it's situated at the end of every sinfully lived life and godless sojourn on earth. To argue against hell with regard to its being spacious enough to accommodate all sinners is to argue against the earth's rotation around the sun given its alarming weight and vastness. Or, turning it other way round, it's to consider the size of the brain and doubt its formidable ability. Or, who will not give kudos to the Almighty Creator when he realizes that this oval-shaped jelly-like structure buried within our skulls, small though, is instrumental to the wonders of the world in communication, medicine, science and technology?

"As these cannot be scientifically disproved, so is hell. Today, as earth accommodates an incredible population of human beings, so does hell accommodate its inmates."

"Alright...Eze, I hope you're not among the aggressive sect who has this false hope and superstition of antiquarians that they are going to heaven sometimes...sometimes?"

"Sir, you mean at Rapture?"

"Yes...yes at the so-called Rapture!"

"Ahm...anyway, I'm among them..."

"A–a–h Eze! What of the Law of Gravity?"

"Sir, Rapture is the hope of all Christians; it's neither superstition nor false hope. And gravitational force has nothing to do with it."

"Rapture? That's piffle!"

"Sir, you mean it's nonsense?"

"It's both nonsense and rubbish!"

"Sir…"

"No! No! I can't agree to that. Eze, no, never! Professor Patrick dismissed."

"I would like to advise that you don't only agree to that but be converted before Christ comes or death knocks."

"Eze, wait! Wait! Are you one of those Homegoer Christians?" Professor Patrick aggressively demanded, pointing to Eze as if it was a crime to be one. "Ah …you'll fail my course. Look, unless you drop that dogma of empty claims, never step this office again nor call my mobile phone. Okay! I said that holding nobody an apology."

"Prof. sorry, I'm still your student no matter what. But, I can't give up my faith. Or, how shall I escape, if I neglect so great Salvation."

"I said you're on your own -- a car parked at owner's risk. I don't know who cares whether you escape or perish. Just walk out with your indiscreet obstinacy and senseless dogma," he pointed him to the entrance. "You're brainwashed. You're misled. You're indoctrinated, in spite of all the psychology and philosophy courses we taught you."

"Sorry Sir!"

"Be sorry for yourself."

Eze went away.

7 - A theatre OF TWO friends

On a Friday, Janet Frank ran into Susie, her old friend, at water stand. Incidentally, Susie herself had recently turned to Jesus in a neighbourhood crusade. Janet who had no other story to tell that time than the dream of Senior Bukky was happy to share the same with Susie.

"Janet! Is it you?" Susie exclaimed in surprise.

"Susie...Susie l–o–n–g time, no see," Janet hollered.

"How are you?" asked Susie as they hugged each other.

"Fine! What of you?" Janet replied

"I'm fine! Great to see you. When did you come from the hostel?" Susie enquired.

"Nearly four weeks ago."

"And you never bothered to say hello to me?"

"I'm sorry."

"How is 'acada'?"

"Not bad Susie."

Susie was busy fetching water as the greetings and exchange of pleasantries were in progress. After some brief discussion, Susie was ready to go.

"Janet, I'm going. I mustn't be late. I'll check you tomorrow, God willing."

"E-e-m Susie, before you go, I have something important to share with you briefly. I wouldn't take much of your time, please."

"What's that?" Susie asked curiously, as she put down her pail of water.

"You see, in the very morning of our vacation, one Senior Bukky whose bed is next to mine in the hostel dreamt that Jesus was coming to take away the truly converted souls of the earth to heaven any moment from now. This is in accordance to the Book of First Corinthians chapter 15 verses 51 and 52 that say: *'Behold*

I show you a mystery; we shall not all sleep, but we shall be changed. In a moment, in the twinkling of an eye, at the last trump: for the trumpet shall sound, and the dead shall be raised incorruptible, and we shall be changed.' I wish you heard the story directly from her, you'll know it's true. She explained that any girl still keeping a sin partner known as *boyfriend* would not make the Rapture. Not only that, girls who are into homosexual practices and those that burn their hairs and bleach their skin for beauty sake with those that put on men's wears like trousers or others who expose their nakedness through indecent dressing, however religious, will be disqualified on this day we're talking about.

"Girls and female teachers who're involved in abortion or those who steal or cheat in exams with those who employ abusive language will be left behind when the trumpets of God sound. Immediately I heard this, my heart pricked me. I could not help it than to ask for forgiveness in the name of Jesus the Son of God. God forgave me and changed my life. Now, I have that assurance of going with Him whenever he comes."

Susie's face beamed with joy.

"I can see you smiling; are you too saved from sin, Susie?" Janet asked in surprise.

"I thank the Lord, Janet; I'm also converted by the grace of God."

"You mean it? When? Tell me your experience!"

"Anyway, sometimes ago, a neighbour just invited me to a crusade rally at the Amusement Park organized by Gospel Light Mission. The preacher's sermon that night was '**You Will Give Account**.' The sermon convicted me, troubled me beyond mouth could tell it. I cried for the years wasted in sin. I bowed my head and pleaded for mercy. I told Jesus to come into my heart. From that evening, I have had peace, freedom from all sins and bad habits."

"Thank God for you Susie. May he uphold us till the end?"

"Amen," Susie answered.

"But then we have to tell others. Susie, I don't know whether you notice that these are days of religion without the life of Christ. So many youths go to church, carry Bibles, but have no new life experience. In the corridor of religion outside there are many young people like us, who, of course, are talented youths zealous for church activities. But good many of them are only floating on religious crest without any encounter with conversion. Should we be silent until they pass away without heaven?"

"No!" Susie replied.

"Such are bound to be disappointed on that great day..."

"It's true, Jane."

"Please, lest I forget, have you told your Uncle?"

"Which one?"

"Hun...Uncle Harry," Janet combed her memory to recall the name.

"Oh, I remember he taught you in the primary school," Susie recalled.

"He used to be my class teacher both in primary four and six."

"Uh...Jane, Uncle Harry has a terrible problem now."

"A terrible problem? What's it?"

"He has a liver problem," saying it in a low tone.

"A liver problem? Whao! How managed?"

"We don't know what really caused it."

"What a pity," Janet tapping her fingers.

"Don't tell anybody please," Susie pleaded.

"Okay. But can we visit him?"

"Why not? We can. But we pray it doesn't happen...

"What's it?"

"Doctors have said he may pack up any moment from now."

"No, we reject that for him in Jesus' name. But then is he converted?"

"No."

"Ah, then we must quickly do something about that Susie."

"Like what?"

"We must visit him. Apart from praying for his healing, we must introduce the Saviour to him. That is the greatest role we can play in his eternal existence beyond the grave, in case.... Susie do you understand me; although nobody prays so?" declared Janet.

"Of course yes!"

"Susie, please, it has to be tomorrow because if Uncle Harry dare pass away like that without we telling him about settling his sin matter with God, I doubt if heaven will forgive us. Besides, in the new world to come, the redemption blood will forever declare that we incurred a loss for God's project in our lifetime whenever God's eyes behold those who slipped into hell by the negligence of those that didn't warn them."

"That's terrible, Jane. Anyway, where do we meet?"

"I'll come to your house at 10 am. It's from there we go to the hospital."

"Alright...bye bye."

Janet and Susie parted with the promise to visit Uncle Harry in the hospital the next day to urge him to accept Jesus lest he dies in his sins and, beyond the grave, faces what is worse than a liver problem.

Since Mr. and Mrs. Frank discovered Janet's new found faith, they had not only withdrawn their love from the girl but had closed down their parent-child relationship. They restricted her movement. A lot of teasing, mockery, insults and complaints that would get her fed up of whether there would be any Rapture or not were being thrown to her each day like a stone. Even, there was a threat that her going back to the hostel was under probability.

Because of all these, Janet felt that taking permission to visit Uncle Harry in the hospital to pray or win his soul for God would appear as one of the 'madness' her parents were talking about in her newly found faith. However, after much restlessness in her spirit, she decided she would write Uncle Harry a letter through Susie who later came to check her at home when she did not see her as agreed.

Here is the copy of the letter she sent to Uncle Harry in the hospital:

At Home

10.15am.

Dear Sir,

How are you now? I hope you're getting better?

Uncle Harry, it is me, Janet Frank, a one-time student of yours at Kite Academy and a friend of your niece, Susie. I was informed of the problem at hand and the present development. I wanted to come in person but I have some restriction at home. I feel so sorry about the matter. It is unfortunate!

However, with humility of heart and bent knees, I counsel that you hand your life over to Jesus immediately you finish reading this hurry-written letter. Jesus is the Healer and the only safe harbour for now especially that the doctors seem to be in their wit's end.

Dear Sir, the greater sorrow after life wouldn't be that someone passed on by a liver infection but that he failed to pray for forgiveness that promises a room in the bosom of Christ. Sir, liver problem or another infection, death must come at least through one way. However, the Bible says, "Blessed are the dead which died in the Lord from henceforth ...that they may rest from their labours; and their works do follow them."

If you can take trouble and settle with Jesus now, when the bell rings and you pass away, angels would come and carry your soul home in glory, where a place of rest from all struggle and pain awaits you.

Sir, if you don't mind, this is how I settled with the Lord, you can follow the same pattern:

1. I closed my eyes
2. I confessed my sins to God

3. I said, "God forgive me through Jesus, your Son, whom I accept now as my Saviour and Lord. Register me in your book as one of your saints. Come and abide in me from now".

4. I pledged an unbroken determination in my prayer that I would not sin again.

Sir, could you just do the same now. I wish you God's overwhelming peace. I am praying to God for you, Uncle, assuredly believing that He will make you whole.

Your student,

Frank Janet

8 - OPPORTUNITY COMES but once

One afternoon, in the household of the Franks, San Hassan, Janet and Grandma were left at home. The three of them sat at the backyard busy chatting. At the period of this story, Grandma was eighty-five years old. A committed member of St. Smith's Church, Grandma had been an instrumentalist right from her youth days. She loved to play violin until, for old age, her hands began to shake on the string. She used to be fond of Janet.

"You'll buy me a new wrist-watch before our resumption, Grandma" Janet requested.

"Janet, tell your daddy to buy you one, I'm old you know."

"Grandma, old people too do have money."

"Only old people who are working," Grandma responded with shaky voice.

"You're right."

"Your Grandma is old, I can't work again."

Suddenly, the thought of Grandma passing away soon struck Janet's mind. Immediately she picked up Grandma on the issue of Senior Bukky's dream.

"Grandma, something happened to a hostel mate of mine before I came home."

"Uhun...," Grandma tuned her hears.

"She woke up from her sleep and said she had seen in her dream that Jesus had come and taken away the Christians. To show that the dream was not just a mere tale, she opened her Bible and showed me where it is written that Jesus will come soon. The Bible challenges Christians in the First Thessalonians chapter 5 verses 1 and 2 when it says:

'But of the time and the season brethren ye have no need that I write unto you. For yourselves know perfectly that the day of the Lord so cometh as a thief in the night.'

"There is a danger for all who are alive today to avoid. The danger is to live but have no life freed from sin. When He comes, only those who're daily living sin-free life will go with him to the new City. Granny, like you who're now old, you would be the luckiest if you are counted fit to go with Him when he comes."

"Before we came to Coveland, the Reverend at St. Smith Headquarters used to tell us the story, but he didn't make mention of any danger whatsoever," Grandma disclosed.

"A–a–h, maybe the Reverend's story is different from this one. There is a great danger for everybody who is a sinner this time around because the coming Lord will appear like a thief. At His arrival, He will invite people for the country he calls the New Jerusalem, but then only those approved by heaven to be living free from sin will take part. The list of their names is with Him in His book called *The Book of Life.* When he comes in the company of his many angels with His supernatural power, He'll call them by trumpet sound. His people will hear Him wherever they are, either in the grave or at mortuary or whether they are sleeping or awake. Immediately, they will disappear from the earth and gather at His feet in the occasion called *the marriage supper of the Lamb*."

"What must we do to be among?" enquired Grandma.

"Granny, to be among, we have to be sorrowful for our past misdeeds which the Bible calls our sins. We are to confess all to God; ask for forgiveness; turn away from them and receive Jesus into our hearts."

"You should tell your Daddy so that all of us can do that at the family altar tomorrow..."

"No, Granny, God reckons with this time when it comes to the issue of repentance. Tomorrow's altar may be too late..."

Janet turned to San Hassan.

"Uncle San, I hope you know this is what I discussed with you on Thursday inside my Daddy's car on our way to the market?"

"Yes, I know. I did as you said when I got home, though initially I had a problem of reconciling the discussion with my religious belief. However, my spirit pressed hard on me to pray about it. After I did, I noticed a change within me."

"Yes, that's it. That's the pardon," confirmed Janet and turned back to Grandma.

"Now, let's pray..."

Grandma and Janet prayed. Though quietly, Grandma settled with God. San committed Grandma to God as well.

They had just finished the prayer when Aunty Patience knocked at the gate. Janet went to answer the door. Aunty Patience was a close relation to the Franks. She was a teacher in one of the primary schools around.

"Good evening Aunty," Janet politely greeted.

Ignoring the greeting, Patience came inside and asked, "Why is everything so quiet?"

"My Mum and Dad are not in, but Granny and Uncle Yisa are there at the backyard."

"You'll greet them for me; I'm in a hurry. I decided to stop over and see you over a matter Daddy complained about. I'm just from one Miss Florence a member of staff in my school. She is seriously ill and her wedding is two weeks away. When we didn't see her in school, I decided to check her at home."

"Has she been to any hospital?"

"Uh...huh yes, yes, she had. That aside, now Janet, Daddy reported you to me that you had joined Christ Home-going Church and you no more wear earrings and had abandoned 'minis' bought for you just in the name of religion? What pained him most which he described as a high profile embarrassment was that you refused to buy him just a bottle of Sunlight Larger Beer. True or false?"

"Aunty, I can't tell you a lie, I haven't been to Home-going Church for once. In the hostel, everybody attends the school chapel. My understanding of the scripture has made me remove those things Daddy mentioned. As for Sunlight Larger Beer, no heaven-bound soul will drink beer either a bottle or more. I will be sending my own father to hell if I bought him beer."

With a frowned face, Florence submitted: "Well, I'm sure you know that I was once a born-again stuff. But when I was persecuted by my Uncle and the community, I had to have a rethink. Now that I wear my necklace, tiny earrings and perm my hair rather than plait it, nobody troubles me again. Janet, let me tell you, I joined this 'S.U' when I was in the Grammar School and this same spiritual meningitis almost killed me but I survived. Fortunately or unfortunately, I picked it up again at the

Teachers' College, where I used to go about with Bible and roam the hostels in the name of evangelism. But today I have learnt to take things with ease. As I now attend our father's church, see, I'm as free as air. Janet, you have to do something about this born-again syndrome. You know, you're a student. Try to avoid too much of it. God himself understands. Can you hear that? Please don't create an unnecessary problem for yourself. I'll be here on Monday to know your decision about it. Okay!"

"Thanks Aunty, but somebody in my hostel, four weeks ago, dreamt that Jesus is coming…"

"Bye bye…keep your idle tale to yourself. Senseless, what are we saying; what's she saying? I don't know who doesn't dream," Patience stepped out in annoyance.

"Please Aunty don't be annoyed. Please, wa–i–t. Ah…she's gone."

Janet was not bothered as such by the 'bite' of Aunty Patience's words, but was disturbed by her backsliding, which was obvious in the way she had spoken.

While Janet closed the gate to go inside, Susie came running and calling Janet's name at a distance. Janet turned back again.

"Susie how…"

"Janet, my Uncle is gone!"

"To where?" Janet greatly worried.

"My Uncle is d–e–a–d…"

"He's wh-a-t?"

"Ja-net, he's d-e-a-d," crying.

"Oh! Death at last?"

"See me oh!" shedding tears.

"Susie, aahahh Uncle Harry is gone." She too burst into crying.

Who will console who as both of them betrayed emotion? They cried for long.

"He has gone to rest." Janet managed to speak, "When did it happen?"

"Early this morning."

"That means the problem had affected him much before taking him to the hospital," Janet complained.

"Not really, you know anything liver could be dangerous," Susie submitted.

"Uh-huh, it's true."

"Ah...my Uncle...," crying again.

"Please take heart, Susie."

"Thanks, Jane..."

"Will he be buried immediately?"

"I don't know yet, but it's likely he'll be embalmed in the mortuary for now until family members meet," Susie replied.

"Did you deliver the letter I sent?"

"I did. I went to the hospital yesterday again to visit him. He was reading his Bible when I got there and felt quite better. In fact during our discussion he told me that he had settled with God and when leaving he said I should greet you and tell you that he had done what you said. And that was only yesterday evening."

"You mean it?"

"Just early this morning at 6.o'clock or thereabouts, his wife came crying that he had given up and had been take

n to the mortuary."

"Esh...," Janet reacted.

They both burst into crying again. Oh, the death of a loved one could really be painful.

9 - EARLIER THAN EXPECTED

In the day of Rapture, when the Lord came to gather the harvest of the earth, and to close the dispensation of grace, it was all like a child's play. It is hard to think of any event ever in human history that is comparable to the catching away of the saints. Rapture, the hope of the nations, the comfort of the persecuted, was an incident that jolted human psyche; gave journalists stories to write and made newspapers sell. It, no doubt, threw procrastinators left behind into late prayers as if that would serve as an antidote.

This is what happened at Coveland, the city in question. For one reason or the other, the resumption to school for the new session delayed for three weeks or thereabouts that year. That made boarders and day students stay put at home with their parents. While they were busy waiting for the government to announce the new resumption date, as holiday makers, most teens got engaged in helping their parents to sell goods downtown Coveland. Others kept on with the usual holiday classes in their neighbourhood. During that period, the persecution of Janet's parents had sufficiently risen to the brim. Nevertheless, the girl had determined not to reverse her footstep from the Lord. A convert of barely two months, Janet had influenced virtually all her neighbours with the good news that only the deaf, who could not hear, could be pardoned for not being told. Many of those she witnessed to accepted, however, some rejected.

In the said day, Rapture day, the day broke quite all right and the world woke up as it used to, but only to realize that real Christians were gone. Surprisingly enough, there was no signal to the event in the previous night. In the night that preceded the incident, music still went on as usual in the beer parlours and restaurants.

And people still scrambled for the best 'suya' (pastrami) at Suya joints in Coveland in the eve of the occurrence. The sky above, in the night before, was on itself, as quiet as ever, and people went to bed as they used to. No owl made a threatening alarm; no moon created any scene of caution. As birthdays were celebrated, so were weddings conducted at different quarters that week with pomp, glitz and glamour. As for fashion, even in the acclaimed new generation churches, half-dressed ladies, some with their micro minis, others with their trousers and coated nails, still marked attendance at the Sunday service that preceded the day. To show that human hearts were no less stuffed with earthly things at the time in question like at anytime in the past, cigarette, beer, money-doubling bureau were yet on advert, even up to the previous day's newspapers. But the rhythm of shock, alarm, crying and questions woke the world in the morning that followed.

Going by the information gathered from those left behind, particularly, the media reporters, the event might have happened in the early morning of the day; although, given differences in the time zone, it was broad day in some others. At any rate, nobody in particular could tell the exact moment of the day and the very minute of the hour it dawned on them. In some big cities in Africa, the day was about breaking for normal business activities, when merchants will dress up for the usual hustle and bustle of the day and the office workers will dash out to join the company staff bus, when the alarm blew in the sky. And behold, all over places, it was disappearing phenomenon. While it was at cold dawn in Australia, the morning broadcast routine was busy engaging the continuity studios in America when the awesome experience befell the world. In Coveland, it was nearing early Morning Prayer time in the Cathedral when the bridegroom came. Some from the Arabian region said that the Imams were on their way to raise prayer in the mosques when the long awaited hope of the nations turned to reality.

The story was the same in the house of the Franks, where morning devotion was a custom. Mr. Frank, the first to wake up that fateful morning checked on Janet in her room for the family devotion, but alas only his daughter's nightgown was on the bed. Appalled by this, Mr. Frank called her wife. The next thing was to check around whether the girl was in the toilet or kitchen. After all effort had proved fruitless, Granny's room was consulted. The same thing had happened to the Octogenarian. The eighty-five years old woman had gone in Rapture as well. The evidence to confirm this reality was her nightgown, which had dropped on the floor. The couple was thrown into a complete state of pandemonium and was beset by a sudden attack of runny stomach, both almost not knowing whether it was a dream or real life experience. They kept asking each other questions on what could have happened to the duo, particularly to the girl who went to bed the previous night with her usual parting words: 'good night Dad.'

Getting to around half past six, the search had sufficiently extended to the neighbourhood. It was near 7.o'clock when the news reached the family that not only Janet and Granny but some other people in the community had also been declared missing, especially the little children.

In the hostels and staff quarters of the University of Coveland, students and members of staff were reported missing. At Centenary hostel where Eze John lived, Godwin and Eze were busy talking early that morning. Suddenly, Eze just turned white as if to say a wall of snow and instantly vanished away and the towel he tied fell off.

"Eze! Eze! Eze!" Godwin shouted.

"What happened...why the noise? Sophia, another hostel mate, dashed out and demanded.

"We were busy talking about departmental tests when a light shone around him and within a split second, he disappeared," Godwin explained.

"No-o-o, Eze went to hide. I am sure he's being funny today." Larry, himself of Centenary Hostel, Room 3, dismissed.

"Funny? No Larry, Eze's body changed and vanished," Godwin reiterated.

"Eze's body changed? Eze that greeted me just some couple of minutes ago," Larry asked in utmost disagreement.

"Look!" Godwin pointed to the towel on the floor. "He wanted to go and bathe, that's the water in the pail," he confirmed.

"Is not this the Rapture Eze used to talk about?" Sophia reminded others.

"Which Rapture? You think it will be this silent? I doubt," Larry replied and mussed away.

Panic and trauma threw the rest hostel mates into confusion as they recollected that Eze had told them so many times, of how sudden the Rapture would be.

10 - SOME will live TO TELL the story

On her way from Florence, Aunty Patience stopped at Frank's house where a crowd of sympathizers was gathered and mourning. Patience was shocked when she saw the concerned mourners sobbing and tapping their feet on the ground.

"Uncle, what's the problem, why this crowd?"

"We're looking for Janet and Mama!" Replied Mr. Frank sobbingly.

"Were they too *raptured*?"

"We don't know!"

"Because as I left home around 6.30 early this morning and passed by that house (pointing to Mr. Ige's house), I heard a shout of someone lamentably calling Ifoma! Ifoma!"

"Which Ifoma?" Mr. Frank asked rising eagerly.

"Ifoma, the girl in my School, daughter of Mr. Henry, the tailor living at Ige's house. But as I was just coming now, I heard that Ifoma disappeared while brushing her teeth outside. People standing by said that recently she claimed to have become converted in one crusade held at the Amusement Park some weeks ago.

"Ifoma Henry also?" Mr. Frank wondered.

"The most shocking of it all is that an eight-day-old baby disappeared in that house too."

"An eight-day-old baby?"

"Uh-huh..."

"Whose baby was that?" Mr. Frank asked.

"Mrs. Henry gave birth last week and today is the naming ceremony. But mysteriously the baby was said to have disappeared from the bed where it was laid," Patience disclosed.

"W-h-a-t? Disappeared? A-a-a-h! Is this the meaning of *'I will come as a thief in the night'*?" putting his finger in his mouth?

"Some church women who came to assist the family in cooking with some elders are still there."

"What of the mother?" Mr. Frank questioned.

"She's there busy crying. Even Mr. Henry, the father, is there bewildered, wondering how his children had vanished away."

"What is this?"

"Our staff member whom I went to visit too has cried and cried like a baby refusing to be consoled. She was the first to tell me it was Rapture of the saints. While I was trying to persuade her to stop weeping and take heart, she declared that she had missed what she had been waiting for since thirteen years ago when she became converted just for the abortion committed five days ago."

"Why abortion?"

"Her wedding is some weeks away and according to her, her church wouldn't conduct a wedding if the bride is found to be pregnant."

"Did the fiancé go?"

"No! He met me there. He too couldn't go in Rapture," Patience narrated.

"And Janet said it, even that a senior in her hostel dreamt about it. But who took her serious?" Mr. Frank lamented.

"No wonder, it was the same thing the girl intended to tell me yesterday, but I snubbed her. Oh, what a mistake!"

These words of regret had hardly come out of Patience's mouth when Pastor Ray Fred dashed inside sweating and panting for reality.

"Is it the same here too?" he exclaimed.

Mrs. Frank staring at him asked, "Pastor Ray, why? You're here too?"

"Uh-oh...all my church members have kept asking me the same question."

"Is he from 'Home-going'?" Mr. Frank demanded from her wife.

"No. He's the Pastor of the popular Daily Showers Interdenominational."

"Okay," nodding his head. "Excuse me Pastor," he continued, "Is it true that the trumpet has blown and the saints have gone?"

"Em... the way things are now, I don't think there is any ground for doubting that. So many little children of members of my church are reported missing. It was the unbearable crying of their parents at my doorstep that forced me out of home."

"Then what is the hope of those of us here?" Mr. Frank asked.

"The truth is that the government of the world will soon become the government of the Antichrist and the Great Tribulation days are ahead."

Soon, people began to leave one after the other, Patience and Mrs. Frank, dumbfounded, sat down. Ray turned to Mr. Frank.

"Chief I will soon be going. Get newspapers or listen to news."

"I'm only waiting for San, my driver, to come and buy me a newspaper."

Pastor Ray, staring strangely at him, asked, "Sir, which San?"

"San Hassan."

"San Hassan of Oak Street, near our church worship centre?" Pastor Ray asked again.

"Uh-huh...," replied Mr. Frank.

"Or, not that Moslem boy?" Pastor Ray asked once again.

"Yes..."

"He's gone too...?"

"Gone to where?"

"I've just passed by his father's house now. So many people are there busy talking about him. They said he was dressing up for work when a light glowed around him, suddenly he disappeared into thin line."

11- WHAT a COSTLY mistake!

Having sustained some respite after he had struggled to curb his feeling of regret and tears that had bathed his eyes for long, Pastor Ray headed for Don Oscar Estate. He went directly to the house of the Abdullahs. Mr. and Mrs. Abdullah used to be an exemplary Christian couple within the estate community. Mr. Abdullah was an employee of Talent Travels Limited in Coveland while his wife, Catharine Abdullah was a matron at Royal Road Hospital before they were both raptured early that morning.

This couple and their two children: Richard and Roseline attended Christ Home-going Church in Coveland. Roseline who had just finished her OND in Marine Polytechnic at Coveland was the first born while Richard who got the State Scholarship a year ago to study Mechanical Engineering abroad, specifically at

Springfield, Massachusetts, was the second. Information had not reached home as to know whether Richard made the Rapture in Springfield or not, but Roseline his elder sister was left behind. At any rate, Richard had a testimony of genuine conversion before he was made children church organist until the time he went to Springfield for study. Roseline, on her own, used to sing solo in the church choir before gaining admission into the polytechnic.

That day, Roseline awoke out of sleep to discover that Mummy and Daddy were nowhere to be found. She combed the house from the bedroom to the toilet and from the store to the car park. She shouted their names. She cried aloud thinking that a gang of armed robbers had invaded the house overnight and killed her parents. But after strict observation, she noticed that the main entrance was intact, not broken. Bewildered, she went into her parents' room repeatedly. Fear and anxiety gripped her because nothing else got missing in the whole building except Mr. and Mrs. Abdullah. She was in that swelling shock and misery when the cry of alarm reached her of a neighbour who disappeared into thin air early that morning while pressing her clothes. Roseline tuned to a radio station. Surprisingly, *rapture* and *second coming of the Lord* were dominating phrases on air. Temper rose and fell in her. She wailed; she lamented for being left behind. Her eyes that were once keen soon became dim and her countenance sad. She tried to carry her Bible, but no, she could not read it. She opened her hymnbook to the popular song she loved to sing anytime her heart was troubled and life seemed to fall apart, but tears blurred her eyeballs and emotion deprived her of tune and rhythm. After she had cried to exhaustion, she sat down at the balcony and leaned her back against the wall as if she were in coma.

On that spot, thought took her on a long excursion to her past when she used to be zealous for the Lord; when she would not joke with sin; the time the Holy Spirit was the guardian of her soul. She remembered perfectly well that she used to be called 'Sister Home-goer' because she would not perm her hair, paint her lips, wear skin-tight belly-exposing blouses not to talk of fixing nails like other 'Christians' around, and rather than being offended when called nickname, she would just smile and go her way. Roseline began to weigh herself on the balance. She soon called back to mind the path she trod in the Grammar School where she practiced Christianity even in the examination hall to the extent that her mates could tell who was born again and who was not. She thought of those good old days when she would use *Our Daily Bread* booklet to answer the questions of her classmates on Bible subjects.

Like a flashback, what overtook her on the narrow road also fell back to her memory in quick succession: how a boy won her heart as if with a charm in OND 1 at Marine Poly. She recalled the first day she secretly tried trousers contrary to her long-held Christian conduct supported by the Holy Book in **Deuteronomy 22 verse 5.** She soon remembered the afternoon she tried lipstick and the day she accepted an offer of kiss from a boyfriend. She did recollect the first love letter she wrote in her life. Roseline could not bear it, she lamentably cried again. As hot tears were busy falling down with a bang from her cheeks, she faintly remembered the hymn of Horatius Bonar which she once sang alone when the going was smooth to her church congregation in a Sunday service before a sermon on Rapture was preached by one of her area pastors. As if played on tape recorder, the tune of the hymn began to roll back solemnly into her heart again:

The church has waited long:
Her absent Lord to see;
And still in loneliness she waits,
A friendless stranger she.

Age after age has gone,
Sun after sun has set,
And still in weeds of widowhood
She weeps a mourner yet.

Come then, Lord Jesus, Come!

Saint after saint on earth
Has liv'd and lov'd and died
And as they left us one by one,
We laid them side by side
We laid them down to sleep,
But not in hope forlorn:
We laid them but to ripen there,
Till the last glorious morn.

Come then, Lord Jesus, Come!

The serpent's brood increases
The powers of hell grow bold,
The conflict thickens, faith is low,
And love is waxing cold.
How long, O Lord our God,
Holy and true and good,
Wilt thou not judge thy suffering Church,
Her sighs and tears and blood?

Come then, Lord Jesus, come!

We long to hear thy voice,
To see thee face to face,
To share thy crown and glory then,
As now we share Thy grace.
Should not the loving Bride
The absent Bridegroom mourn?
Should she not wear the weeds of grief
Until her Lord returns?

Come then, Lord Jesus, Come!

The whole creation groans,

And waits to hear that voice
Which shall restore her comeliness,
And make her saints rejoice.
Come, Lord and wipe away
The curse, the sin, the stain,
And make this blighted world of ours
Thine own fair world again.

Come then, Lord Jesus Come!

Roseline lifted her hands as if to fly away. But it was too late. With intolerable ache, she dabbed hot tears from her eyes over and over again. She was in this mood when Pastor Ray Fred knocked at the gate.

"Good morning here."

"Who is that?"

"Mr. Ray."

"From where?"

"From your neighbourhood."

"Wait please." Roseline went inside, brought the key and opened the gate as her hands trembled slightly.

"Good morning Sir."

"How are you?"

"My Dad and Mum...," Roseline asked in seeming unconsciousness.

"Yes, where are they?" Pastor Ray asked in return."

"I have been looking for them since I woke up."

"H-a-a that means they too are gone!" Exploded Ray.

"To where?" asked Roseline.

"To meet the Lord. Or you don't know that Rapture has taken place?"

"What time did my Lord come?"

"I don't know the exact time, but we just woke up to discover that people are missing here and there.

"What went wrong that I'm left here Lord?" gazing into the air.

"Aren't you Roseline?"

"I am."

"I'm surprised to see you here…"

"Uh-oh…" Roseline sounded. Being in deep regret, she kept looking down.

"Your Daddy used to make favourable mention of you when we worked together at Talent Travel Agency."

"Sir, truly I used to be a Christian but I turned back."

"To what?"

"Well, I went to Marine Poly where I had an OND in Accountancy. Before I gained admission, I was doing fine in the Lord, but the lifestyle within the campus influenced me. The Christian fellowship I joined, on its own, made me lose much of my conviction. Before I knew it, the culture in that gathering had killed those

Christian principles Daddy used to teach us at home. Maybe I couldn't have fallen this far and had the last blood in my spiritual vein drained empty if not for our campus Pastor's wife who came to the altar one Sunday service in one horrible, reddish-brown transparent jumper and lust-advertising lips painted in silver-colour lipstick with long coated nail to match. It was this action of hers that made me conclude that since the way it is in the world is the way it is in the church, what profit have I punishing myself. That is why before long, I grew interest in reading love stories in the dailies and romance magazines, mostly Lady Tempest Love Column. *(In those days, Lady Tempest Love Column was, amongst other things, popular for the way it advertised lust and passion. It was carnal-full and passion-rife, madly romantic, erotic, breeding morally bankrupt world. The stench of immoral pictures and 'cancer' of indecent dressing that greeted one's nostril when one opened to the column was sickening, nauseating and stomach-turning beyond what words could describe. The readers of this column, in the majority, consisted of the habitually half-dressed ladies on campus, entertainment 'idols' and those passion-crazy boys who were notorious for downloading naked women who play sodomy at pornographic web-sites. In spite of the popularity so gained, L. Tempest, as she was being fondly called for short by her fans, had ruined the careers of many of her readers especially the adolescent, with so many of their future dreams being truncated by her love tales. But the so-called modern youths of Coveland seemed not to realize this).*

"The next, my dressing began to change. After a while, I started going to questionable places. To worsen it, before my OND 2, I had started dressing and wearing make-ups like ladies I once preached to in the early years of meeting the Lord. I toned, wore net, jilted boyfriends. Even, my final ND 2 result was not totally by the strength of my brain, I cheated to pass some courses, I 'bought' the rest marks with my body."

"But Daddy used to be proud of you."

"Yes, he didn't know that I did all these. I was deceived to cover up whenever I came home for break," she burst to crying again.

"But when I finished my OND," she continued, "and came back home, I decided to go public," crying. "Uncle, do you know..."

"Know what?"

"That my parents were invited by the Church Council because of me and were asked to pray me to restoration before they could continue as church elders. They begged me; they cried about it; they did so many fasting on the issue. But see me, all their appeals fell on deaf ears. In fact, Richard, my younger brother, tried. He wrote me five different letters from Springfield, but I tore all and burnt them.

"Uh…Roseline enough; it is enough. Your parents really tried for you, but…"

"Sir, please tell me about my parents' whereabouts now?" Roseline enquired with sob and anguish.

"They are now all with the Lord at the Marriage Supper."

"A-a-h! Mummy, you really tried for m-e-e, pardon me that I rejected your good advice," gazing again into the space in tears. "What group would my Daddy belong to there? Tell me Pastor?" she asked Pastor Ray again with beads of hot tears rolling down her cheeks.

"Group? No group, no faction in heaven. Only that those hardworking Christians will be rewarded up there. Those who were lazy in their Christian service will watch their work burn."

"Ah, upon all the past warnings," Roseline regretted as she plucked and threw on bare ground her earrings and long artificial nails. "You're part of what hindered me...," she concluded.

"Roseline, you have to take heart and try to listen to news at noon. I want to go back home. I'll check you tomorrow."

Because it was an emergency time, things moved fast. There were tales; there were rumours; there were stories from Timbuktu.

12- TELECAST and MEDIA reports

The topic of the time continued to remain 'Rapture' and the theme for discussion 'missing saints'. By afternoon, the saints' disappearance of that early morning had sufficiently ushered in something akin to pandemonium as lots of propagandas and speculations on the world new government soon to seize power had begun to give those left behind worries and anxiety. The growing tide of missing people cut across all places from cosmopolitan cities to metropolitan areas and down to the rural setting. Armies of sympathizers doted the homes of those whose either parents, children or loved ones were missing.

At 12 O'clock, the world news was on air at Coveland T.V. Frank tuned to the station and listened to the broadcast.

"Good afternoon everyone,

Here is the world news from **Coveland   TV**,

Read by **Willy Carter**,

First, the major items:

*Mysterious disappearance of countless number of people is reported nationwide.

*Ocean of tombs is left open all over the world.

*Babies disappear in hospitals and maternity centres.

*Coveland metropolitan hospitals call for more beds as doctors can no longer accommodate the injured.

*Many plane crashes are reported around the world.

*African countries declare a state of emergency.

*The World Central Government takes over any moment from now.

Now, the news in full:

The world has witnessed a shocking experience following the disappearance of a huge number of people into the thin air early this morning.

According to our correspondents in Africa and Europe, vast majority were preparing for work while some were yet in bed, when they vanished in a twinkle of an eye. It was gathered that all the disappearing folks were from the Christians fold.

MicLeonard of the Information Unit, World Peace Keeping Agencies Headquarters, in an interview this morning, declared that millions of tombs had been broken open with nobody inside them, and while corpses had vanished in mortuaries, countless children had been declared missing all over places.

According to him, all the peacekeeping agencies throughout the globe had reported the incident as being extra-terrestrial, as all efforts to calculate the number of the missing people via satellite was a total fiasco.

He said, on quote "No scientific discovery can refute this as being the act of God, as all findings via modern technology cannot help in any slightest means. As such, it must be the complete fulfilment of the event known as RAPTURE, which the Holy Bible calls the sudden arrival of Jesus Christ to withdraw his saints from the earth. The incident the Holy Book has said should happen unannounced," end of quote.

Owing to the several motor accidents caused by the disappearance of bus drivers in the Coveland metropolitan region, doctors have been seeking for more hospital beds. The reported disappearance which was said to have drastically reduced the number of doctors and nurses available at present in the hospitals has led to the abandonment of the injured crowd. As a result, the incident may shoot up the mortality rate globally, particularly in the United States.

The world news is reaching you from Coveland T.V.

While many plane crashes have been reported in a number of places following the mysterious disappearance of pilots while in flight, the same missing saga has it that a ship captain from Great Lagoon Shipping Company, Derby Road, U.K. was raptured early this morning. The captain, who was reported by most of the crews to be a genuine Christian believer, disappeared just as the ship was ready to sail from the harbour.

The report added that many passenger ships, cargo ships and super tankers expected to arrive ashore this morning were nowhere to be found. Therefore, the Ports Authority with Shipping and Transport Management is quite bewildered by this mysterious incident.

To prevent crime due to the current state of the nation, many African countries have called for a state of emergency to establish peace and security. According to our correspondent in Nigeria, the step becomes necessary as nations are littered with automobiles, fanciful buildings and billion naira worth of properties belonging to the disappearing folk.

Speaking in an interview after the Rapture incident of this morning, the Archbishop of Coveland has confirmed the withdrawal of some Christians from the globe. According to the cleric, the occurrence was to usher in the World Central Government, which would adopt the same system of education, currency and constitution with the mark of citizenship, "666" when she takes global control. He pointed out that all the Heads of State would become subject to the World Central Government immediately she comes to power in order to ensure territorial safety and economic survival of the world, owing to the present global political insecurity coupled with the disappearing phenomenon.

Nations' armed forces in the nearest future are to operate under the single control of the World Central Government. This was his own submission, General Karl, the Commandant of the 12 battalion soldiers in Coveland. Speaking with our correspondent this morning, the Commandant said that the step was to help the new world administration gain full support and deal with anybody wanting to refute her order.

To end the news, another look at the highlights:

*Mysterious disappearance of countless

  people is reported world-wide.

*Ocean of tombs is left open all over the world.

*Babies disappear in hospitals and maternity centres.

* Coveland metropolitan hospitals call for more beds, as wards can no longer accommodate the injured.

* Many plane crashes are reported around the   world.

* African countries declare a state of emergency.

* The World Central Government takes over any moment from now.

     That ends the world news.

We shall bring you further information reaching our station in our ½-hour broadcast at 3. o'clock, stay tuned.

There was silence in the living room for a period, as a result of the same trend of worry and anxiety that had refused to loosen its grip on the viewers.

13- UP FROM the MORTUARY to the sky

Around 5.00pm that day, Larow Harry, the wife of late Ben Harry, the Uncle of Susie, received a phone call from the Niger Mortuary Director to report immediately in company of a friend.

Up until the time of Ben Harry's death, Larow had never given him enough attention and cooperation of a supportive wife. Rather than living Harry in the position where the Divine had placed him as the head of the family, Larow would prefer to display obvious sorrow that sounds like her name for ever getting married to a primary school teacher. That is why she often overrode him and worked down on him even in the presence of her friends. Admitted, she was from a rich home and fortunate as a fresh graduate to have picked up her first job ever in a highbrow advertising company with a car to match. Notwithstanding, she should not have treated the father of her children as a scum of the society. Besides that, Larow still lived her life as when she was not married. With a three-year old marriage, she still did not see anything bad in snapping pictures all about the bar beach and pubs while wearing questionable attires and sitting amidst other men and, sometimes, on their laps.

Sister *Larowee,* as fondly called by little children in her church, was always present for the Sunday service. But for weekly meetings, her answer remained "the spirit is willing but the flesh is weak". Her job weighed a ton in her heart but Bible weighed a straw, therefore, job first. Who could correct such secular abnormality of an articulate advertiser? The worst of it all was that Larow's philosophy of Salvation rested on how hard one could try. Because, according to her, no one could be free from sin. Little wonder, she always muttered some casual prayer of forgiveness whenever her advertising rigmarole allowed her to join her husband and children in the sitting room to chorus: 'O*ur father who art in heaven*...'each morning. As a sequel to the unsettled home and troubles brewed often times by Larow, Harry's problem was compounded when he fell sick that rather than recovering from a mere stomach disorder, the abdominal discomfort degenerated to liver infection, which sent him packing quite untimely.

It was unbelievable when the director of the mortuary narrated the story of what had happened to the corpse of Late Ben Harry to her wife, Larow and Agnes her friend.

"Madam, you're welcome," the mortuary director greeted.

"Yes Sir," replied Larow.

"You have to take heart Madam. Nobody is immune against death. We're all birds of passage. Therefore, one day we must answer our own call. Please don't be sorrowful. May the Lord be with you and the children your husband left behind?"

"Amen," answered Larow in a lonely tone.

"Madam, before I say why you were invited, may I know whether you came alone?"

"No. A friend accompanied me down," Larow answered in a faltering voice of shaky lips.

"Let her come inside."

Larow went to the outer office and returned immediately with Madam Agnes.

"Welcome Madam."

"Good evening," Madam Agnes greeted.

"Evening, thank you. Please have your seat. Now, I want to say we're very sorry to disclose the sad news and mysterious experience of the moment. Going by the information I have with me here, your dear husband, Mr. Ben Harry, a primary school teacher at Kite Academy and resident of 3, Labour Crescent, Coveland Park, passed on to glory last week, precisely 15th of this month at the General Hospital and had since then been embalmed in this mortuary. Am I right?" he raised his gaze and with his heavy bifocal glasses looked at Mrs. Harry at the face for an answer.

"Yes Sir," Larow Harry answered in haste, looking pale and inquisitive.

"Last night the mortuary was intact. The workers on duty were around and, of course, in their duty posts. However, the workers disclosed that early this morning there was a shake in the building and a strange light suddenly descended from nowhere. As they said, just immediately after the light, some of the corpses in the hall appeared to be moving somehow. Because of fear, those workers on duty couldn't move closer to see what was happening. However, when they later had the courage to do, they discovered that some of them had vanished without a trace.

"Initially, the management disregarded the report and arrested those workers with immediate effect thinking that they had connived with some dubious cannibals to steal away the bodies, until the news reached us that it was Jesus Christ who had come suddenly to withdraw all his own - both the dead saints and the living ones. We never still agreed to that claim nor took it as real evidence until we heard the World News Broadcast on Cable Network confirming it. In fact, the story is in *Coveland Times;* the director stretched forth the paper to Larow to read for herself.

"Sir, I don't understand you. How do you mean?" Larow questioned.

"I am saying that, by the list before me, our late Mr. Harry too is missing from the mortuary.

"Mi-what? H-a-a-h," Larow jumped up and rushed out of the Director's Office to the mortuary building, her

friend, Madam Agnes, running after her. Indeed, it was a
baffling experience!

14- GATHERED at the MARRIAGE supper

By evening, streets in Coveland had been literally taken over by newspaper vendors. Local and foreign evening papers had reported the incident with suffocating details. Captions on Rapture graced the front pages of most of the newspapers. Of course, no other lead story for that evening edition beside the Rapture event. Few among so many captions were: 'The Greatest Mystery Ever'; 'His Kingdom Comes Without Observation'; 'His Day Breaks Without Notice'; 'Grace Days Are Over; Antichrist's Era is Near'; 'Sinners in Zion Are Afraid'. Most pictures in the papers were of friends and neighbours who, in dumb surprise with parted lips and straining eyes, were gazing into the sky as if their missing relations were somewhere in the cloud for them to see. Besides this, newspapers pages were full of interviews conducted by news reporters with left-behind evangelists and preachers who, before Rapture, were mushrooming on the world religious landscape. Heart-touching occurrences about the *raptured* saints were also highlighted.

Roseline Abdullah went to nearby street and purchased four different evening papers: *Coveland Times, Echo News, Intelligence Daily* and *National Times*. She rushed back home to read for herself. She began with the *National Times* that had the Rapture story in the front page of that morning issue under the caption, *"Agony of the left-behind."* This is the story:

The world, at the early hours of this morning, experienced the highest scenario of disaster ever following the disappearing of Christians across the curves and corners of the world. Following the incident, series of mass destructions had been reported nationwide. Reports have it that no man-made or natural catastrophe in history is comparable to the woes that hit the nations after the saints' withdrawal. The death toll is alarming but difficult to describe in figure as search goes on in cities and countryside to ascertain who is raptured and who is the victim of the tragedy that followed.

One of the major misfortunes today took place in the ancient city of Marlow near the Defence Ministry, as a naval aircraft on official tour to Benson City crashed in a pancake landing, following the disappearance of the pilot. The casualties numbered forty.

A similar aviation disaster had been witnessed in the Gulf of Coveland beside Extrafo City when a Boeing 747 from one of the African countries crashed on a 21-storey building killing one hundred and thirty-two passengers and eighty people from the building. The accident was attributed to the shock sustained by the pilot on the ground that he was left behind at the Rapture while some passengers on board vanished away.

Tragedy had also greeted Afro Ultra-modern Hospital in the North of Wiwino when its chartered air bus caught fire, burning to ashes its pilot and the ill-fated passenger. The passenger who was said to be on appointment for kidney operation in India resorted to shouting when the doctor on board with him suddenly disappeared while they were busy discussing. The shout was said to have impaired the attention of the reportedly hypertensive pilot who suddenly became non-compos-mentis. Consequent on that, the plane drifted into the thick forest eighty kilometres north of Wiwino and perished.

Motor accident had also claimed many lives early this morning, rendering homes fatherless and forcing many a woman into widowhood. Between Palace Eatery and Marine Polytechnic of Coveland, two luxury buses on tour had a head on collision when one of the drivers indefinitely disappeared while the bus was on motion. The casualties numbered fifty-nine.

New Era Transport Service had a similar story of misfortune to tell this morning as two of its 14-passenger buses on tour to the East of Ezemo in the neighbouring of Sia lost control. The accident, which was consequent to the disappearing factor, claimed sixteen lives and spared twelve heavily injured ones. The two buses were a complete write-off.

Town Council should not forget that indiscriminate dumping of human remains and the disaster's victims could turn to an outbreak of epidemic. As such, the government should help put necessary action into place to prevent this."

Roseline dropped the paper and took the Echo News.

The lead story in the Echo News that day had the headline **'Peter Akinade Shifts Stage to Heaven'** and it went like this:

Peter was the Editor-in-Chief of Revolution Daily, one of the widely circulated papers of the time. The paper used to be toast of the reading public because it used to reveal whatever happened in the House of Assembly to what unfolded in the Safari Park. It had fed the world with events in African States from sports to politics, from business to religion and from agriculture to wildlife. Before its ban, Revolution Daily used to advocate unrestricted press freedom and did display objectivity, impartiality and profundity in its style of reportage. Nine months ago, Revolution Daily published an article under the headline 'Our Holy Egypt'. Felix Audu, the writer of the article, was not out to castigate Egypt as a country neither did he satirize the government on her seat of power. Rather, the content of his essay only assessed the governments of most African States and declared that many were merely recycling of leadership; the issue the writer called 'Episode of Tragedy'. In his observation, Audu established that recycling of leaders would make a supposed hero to turn to zero and the nation's future would melt to shadow. According to him, the idiosyncrasy of African leaders in staying put in the government villa even when the leadership potential has run dry is uncalled for. The essayist brought his satire to a high point when he took trouble to draw a broad antithesis between African leaders and their counterparts in the developed countries.

Audu, who thought that the truth of his 'thesis' would be made obvious by drawing examples from home, called the attention of his readers to the government of the country where Revolution Daily, the paper he was writing for, was being published. The erstwhile President of the country in question had overstayed in office before handing over to one of his political apologists, who, at present, is not doing better. The integral part of this writer's claim leaned, however, strongly to the side of change in the system of governance in African states with his facts falling into the heart as gently as snowflakes. However, this bold satirist, towards the end of his essay, challenged those in power to rule well.

The article raised dust and generated bad blood in the government house. It was labelled an affront to the incumbent government. Therefore, with immediate effect, Revolution Daily was banned but all effort to arrest Felix Audu who wrote the essay was fruitless. Five days later, Peter Akinade, the Editor-in-Chief, was arrested. A cheerful speaker, possessing soft mien and oblong physiognomy, no moustache, no beard, Peter went to cell untried. He was a Christian by faith and lifestyle. He was calm even when the 'flame' was rising and falling over the issue of the article - 'Our Holy Egypt'.

In the early morning of today, as reported by one of our correspondents who interviewed Peter's fellow inmates, he was observing his morning prayer as usual when the prison's atmosphere changed and, all of a sudden, Peter disappeared. We are yet to know the condition of his wife and two children.

Roseline shook her head in awe and dropped the paper.

Public executions are gory sights, when the condemned say their last prayers before bullets tear them in pieces. Often times, their remains are packed together for mass burial. Spots of such pit where the remains of those publicly killed by firing squad or gallows are dumped may be found all over countries of the world. However, only the uniform men know the locales.

Aside this, there are certain occasions when the innocent go to the grave with the culprit or permit me to say that not all those condemned and executed as robbers are truly robbers. Neither are all those accused of coup plotting are really coup plotters. However, they face the wrath of gun either for miscarriage of justice or because the innocent have no helper. We cannot say with certainty which of these factors underlined the case being reported in relation to the Rapture of that morning by the *Intelligence Daily* under the headline '**The Trial of Constable**'. Roseline opened to page five of the paper and read the account with undivided attention. Here goes the story:

Three weeks ago at Regina City, seven top military officers were arrested with three police officers and one Constable for making an attempt to bomb the President's jet at the airport. The Constable who had just been posted to the airport four days to the incident, and who was innocent of the plot was handpicked by the officers that morning to set the wire bomb on some designated areas on the tarmac where the craft would land. The Constable, we are told, obeyed the senior officers not only for the military axiom of 'Obey the last order', but because the bomb was so branded in such a way as to be mistaken for the flexible wire of a public address system.

By and large, the attempt failed and the plotters were arrested. A martial court that tried them and found them guilty of coup plotting gave them death sentence by firing squad. On the day of their execution, chained together in threes, they were driven in Black Maria to the spot where their stakes awaited them. Met with hundreds of eyes of the members of public, they moved to their stakes with bowed heads. While some spectators hissed continually, others muttered shameful utterances at them. After a hymn and their last prayer, they were tied to the stakes. The firing squad, which could not be recognized because of the mode of dressing, jumped down from the motorcade. They took their positions and waited for the last order. Less than five minutes later, the order went out and the squad released fusillade of gunshots on them. The bullets shook them; stretched them and tore them. They immediately surrendered to the cold fang of death. The sight was horrible.

Immediately, they were packed away to be dumped in a pit somewhere behind Area X Police Station at Regina City. Around 5:30 this morning the pit broke open as if by earthquake and some people resurrected out of the pit which, as gathered by our correspondent, had accommodated corpses in their hundreds for over four decades. However, who and who resurrected belong to the divine.

Roseline, again, shook her head in sorrow and put the paper aside.

The paper she read last was the *Coveland Times*. Its lead story for that day issue was headlined, **'Death: where is thy Victory?'** The story opened with a quotation from Addison's work: **'The Tombs in Westminster Abbey'**.

When I look upon the tombs of the

great, every emotion of envy dies in me;

when I read the epitaphs of the

beautiful, every inordinate desire goes out;

when I meet with the grief of

parents upon a tombstone, my

heart melts with compassion;

when I see the tomb of the parents

themselves, I consider the vanity

of grieving for those whom we

must quickly follow; when I

see kings lying by those who

deposed them, when I consider

rival wits placed side by side, or

the holy men that divided the world

with their contests and disputes,

I reflect with sorrow on the little

competitions, factions, and debates

of mankind. When I read the several dates of the tombs -

of some that died yesterday and some six hundred

years ago - I consider that great

day when we shall all of us be

contemporaries, and make our

appearance together'.

Some metres away to the Old Cathedral Church of Coveland was the church cemetery where those saints from missionary era till date were buried. Very close to the small gate that led to this silent ground was a big board mounted where it is written in one of the Coveland dialects:

'These all died in faith…' And 'Precious in the sight of the Lord is the death of his saints'.

Among those committed to the mother earth in that solitary ground was Reverend Sunday Mile-End. Mile-End brought the gospel to Coveland in the 1820s, worked tirelessly with Elder Longfellow who, reportedly, was his first convert. Longfellow, who worked as a primary school teacher then but later died in a shipwreck during one of their outreaches to the waterside area, used to earmark half his salary for the work, especially for the caring of the converts and persecuted brethren. Through this, Rev. Mile-End, a diligent missionary, was able to achieve much in those days that the light of truth spread in Coveland like wild fire, and souls were saved in their dozens. History has it that Sunday Mile-End died four days after laying the foundation stone of Coveland Cathedral Church at the age of ninety six having spent many years of active missionary service in Coveland.

Mile-End remains were laid to rest in the Cathedral's Cemetery. However, before the seeming earthquake that broke open his tomb this morning, part of the tomb itself had already cracked and part had fallen because it was long since he had been buried there. Sources said that the inscription on it, like the date and the epitaph were no longer legible for eyes to capture. This is because some letters had dropped while some had been shrunk away by some weeds that had grown on the cracked tomb. The cemetery was sloppy in topography; this affords a person at the south gate of the Cathedral to see the ruined tomb far away in the midst of weeds.

After Mile-End's departure to his final home to rest, it appeared his spirit never broke ties with the Cathedral in that the subsequent ministers of this missionary church took after Rev. Mile-End and built on what he established before he went away. The way he did things was always a reference manual for each succeeding overseer that the new generation of the church was not alien to its source and members often wished they had been born during the period their Father-in-the-Lord, Rev. Mile-End, was alive.

Gathered from a reliable source, after the Rapture this morning, some elders who were left behind went to the vicarage to confirm the reality of the occurrence lest it was mere propaganda. Unsatisfied with the vicarage information, they crossed over to the cemetery to see if any of their late brethren had resurrected as had often been said at their burial that they had gone to rest at the Saviour's bosom till the morning of resurrection. On getting there, surprise seized them and hardly could they talk to one another when they saw that really tombs were flung open, but only few. Disappointment greeted their minds, their mood become dull increasingly as the tombs of many of those they had buried with grand Christian wake-keeps, well-attended services of songs and befitting burial ceremonies remained as sealed as they have been. They went ahead and checked whether their first Overseer, Rev. Sunday Mile-End, also resurrected. On getting there, his tomb was open and completely empty.

Some other people who resurrected in the church yard of Coveland Cathedral were Madam Lai Craig who died on the 4th August 1903; Capt. Joseph Peatle (Rtd) who died in 1853; Josiah Humphreys who died in January 1920 but the tomb of his wife who died in 1931 did not open. Those that also resurrected were Raymond Eke who died on 10 March 1886; Elder Jacob Anslem who died in a motor accident on June 3, 1915 and Barrister Leonard Adams who died 1900 at 87.

Coveland Times concluded the story by saying, **"Certainly, Rapture was no more a myth."**

15 - ANTICHRIST! JUST AT THE corner

Roseline fell on her knees and prayed for restoration. She started by confessing her backsliding to God. She prayed and prayed but assurance for forgiveness seemed difficult for her to regain.

"Where is my Saviour?" she cried. However, salvation appeared hard for her to receive. All the same, she continued, though in hopeless misery.

For those who made the Rapture and have gone with the Lord, their life-chapters are closed but what do we suppose will happen to those left behind, especially Pastor Ray Fred, Patience, Larow, Roseline and Dave Pauli all of who played the unwise virgins and who, of course, would soon witness the Antichrist's reign of terror. Who among them will endure the shriek or manage the panic? Who can endure the heartless torture, the toughest agony, the painful persecution with unlawful detention and incarceration? Because soon now, the mark of the Antichrist, '666', will be made mandatory for all residents of Coveland as for all those who did not go with the Lord in Europe, Asia, Australia, North America, South America, Africa and Antarctica. *'And he causeth all, both small and great, rich and poor, free and bond to receive a mark in their right hand, or in their foreheads: And that no man might buy or sell, save (except) he that had the mark, or the name of the beast or the number of his name. Here is wisdom. Let him that hath understanding count the number of the beast: for it is the number of a man; and his number is Six hundred threescore and six (666)'* Rev.13:16-18

Though, the saints had gone to be with the Lord, some saints' neighbours, relatives and families like Mr. and Mrs. Frank, Ifoma's parents, Roseline Abdullah and Mr. Hassan were left behind in the City of Coveland. Those who were left behind must exist; of course, the world will still exist after the Rapture. As such, those who missed the Rapture like Roseline, Dave Pauli, Larow, Patience, and Pastor Ray Fred still lived on. Now, what happened to them when the reign of terror began is the question. What befell them when they were confronted by the choice between '666' and death is a matter of great concern. What did they do? Did they go for the mark of the Antichrist or opt for death by being brutally murdered or by being electrocuted? Could they endure the ferocious period or they compromised by accepting the mark and were doomed forever? When hunger became so unbearable and thirst was severe, did they prefer to die as Tribulation saints or receive the number of the Antichrist in their foreheads? Who among them could stand this last chance, though by his own blood? And who tried but could not make it?

PART TWO - Antichrist's 666

16 - THE UPDATE

Since the Rapture took place and the saints of God were taken up yonder, the face of things had changed all over places. The circle of time, like a drama, had weaved itself around people throughout the world. For days, radio announcements were dominated mainly by the same missing syndrome. News and reports aired daily followed the same trend.

As it was with most countries of the world - developed and the Third World - Coveland society too had shifted at all levels of what used to be her norms, just after the saints' ascension. Take for instance, the peace and emotional stability of her citizenry had escaped into obscurity; another way of saying that her defence had cascaded and her security had hit a rock. Not surprising then that a great mass of her members of public now crouched low in deep feeling of insecurity. Her economy, as will soon become apparent, was not in itself a sacred cow. It had been messed up to an inconceivable extent that hunger made itself a daily companion of many homes. As parents were chased about by what to eat as well by how to make do with the chaos and trauma of the time, little children on the other hand were abandoned at home by their mothers who scouted about for food. This answered why children born around that period were underfed, and were often neglected at home. Of course, the same gave the reason behind their emotional deprivation, withered intellect, depression and low self esteem. Or who could believe that such notable market and bubbling emporium, Meridian Square, would soon be shut down. But a year ago, it would appear inadmissible if anyone had told residents of Coveland that they would suffer from bitter hunger. Such prediction would have fallen on a deaf ear, given the nation's level of development and enormous resources under her control.

Any way, in fulfilment of the scriptures, the Great Tribulation - commonly referred to as *Daniel's 70th Week* - commenced in those days with full force. While it kicked off, troubles ballooned along unchecked. As for the menace of the pseudo-man of peace, *a.k.a* Antichrist, that one flourished without restraint. Killing was rampant; arrest was raging; peace was in great want as economy was awkward at best. For absence of rest of mind, people's experience from one nation to another really confirmed that it was, indeed, the time of **Jacob's Trouble**.

The period in question was apparently a time of unparalleled desolation for the world, most in particular for countries within European and Mediterranean regions. War, famine, mass destruction of life with high mortality rate overtook the earth following the opening of the first four seals of the scroll mentioned in chapter six of the Revelation Book of the Holy Bible, releasing respectively a white horse with a rider – in person of the Antichrist; a red horse with a rider – in person of the man of war; the black horse with a rider standing for famine; and a pale horse representing death.

Government Reserved Area, GRA, in Coveland was just about two kilometres away to Meridian Square. At Meridian Square, in Coveland City, luxury stayed put. Cars of all brands moved in and out on its cobblestone road. Its mosaic floor of Italian marble was hard and noisy under foot. Chain stores, trendy shops, boutiques and shopping complexes dealing in expensive wears were too many to mention. Hardly was anything money can buy that was ever out of stock in Meridian Square, a confirmation that people of all tastes and aversion patronized it. And given the way thousands of people walked in and out of its gate, I guess you would not accuse me of exaggeration if I say that hunger may whip the members of public to death should Meridian Square be closed down for just twenty four hours; the fact that further unfolds its economic contributions, besides its other desirable human benefits. Meridian Square had its own police. This was aimed at curbing human excesses and carrying out arrest on people engaging in mischievous acts or outright robbery within the Square. Her Fire Brigade was the most prepared ever with twenty-four hour service and well trained fire fighters that could dare a raging inferno.

At any rate, since the saints' withdrawal from the earth, things, by and large, had changed from what they used to be at the square. It was not only sellers that had decreased but buyers too had tapered off, which was the obvious reason for sharp drop in commercial activities generally, with buying and selling having been badly affected.

It was in this deep ocean of trouble in that world of heartache and heartbreak that Mrs. Frank, mother of beloved Janet, had to live in. May be I should tell you, I guess you do not know this, that Madam Frank used to have a shop inside Meridian Square and traded in children's toys. An accomplished trader, she had a fleet of customers. Usually, from twenty fifth of each month in those days of grace when Rapture had not occurred, GRA people, mostly nursing mothers, would hardly allow a space for legs in her shop, just to tell you the level of customers' patronage of her business. They would literally make the shop so busy as if nothing else existed to buy with money than walkers, teddy bears, baby walkie talkie, toy guns and children telephones. It is convenient telling you that Frank was a name synonymous with children toys within Meridian Square.

When the Rapture took place and Janet her only child went away to meet her Lord, a wide gap was left behind for Mrs. Frank's toys customers and fellow Meridian marketers to tell stories. Her child's case was real evidence that ruled off all doubts and guesses regarding the reality of the Lord's second coming. For days, Frank's residence was visited by friends and sympathizers from the Square. At the end of the day, Mrs. Frank became a subject of common conversation so much that whenever she walked into the Square, her presence would attract attention, and people who knew her would point fingers to her for others who did not as the mother of the only child that went to heaven when the trumpet sounded, living mother and father behind.

The scripture cannot be broken, whereas few people had been taken, many had been left behind. A great separation had indeed occurred! It was not a myth that Janet, the only child of Mr. and Mrs. Frank, had been taken too, but her parents were left behind. It was chaotic for them when the era of the man of sin began. The question remains, in what manner do we expect this couple to continue their lives in those terrible days? How would the world around them look like? Would it taste fine or insipid? Chapters ahead provide you with reactions and responses.

17 - THE REGRET

While weeks passed so quickly that time and days sped off in the haste of seconds, dots of mystery were being nurtured in the memory of those left behind. Those unprepared Christians from various denominations in Coveland City, like Coveland Cathedral Church, Coveland Full Gospel Assembly, Pastor Ray Fred's Daily Showers Interdenominational to mention just a few, who missed the great event were busy seeking the way of escape.

One Wednesday afternoon, a postman brought a letter to the Abdullah's residence addressed to Roseline Abdullah by his brother, Larry, from Springfield. Fortunately, the postman met Rose at home who collected Larry's letter with some feelings of relief, thinking she was not altogether a loser. After all, as she thought, she was not only having a relation left behind in the world to share her pain with, but even her own younger brother, her very blood, Larry. With nervous fingers, Rose hastily tore the envelope open in the way she had never done to any of her brother's piece in the past. Her ribs shrank a size when she opened the two-page letter and her sharp piercing eyes fell on the date of writing being pre-Rapture. That is, Larry had posted the letter before the Rapture occurred. It, no doubt, dawned on Rose that the letter had suffered late delivery due to the general state of things in the country at that moment. Sweat, like beads, rose on her forehead and was busy rolling down as she went through the letter. Larry had written in his characteristic manner of pleading, such that Rose had no room for doubting the boy's chance of making the Rapture. His message to his sister maintained the usual heading: **Sister Rose, Just About Your Restoration**. Larry challenged again and again. As if he had foreseen the vision of that Rapture beforehand, he pleaded over and over with Rose to turn away from her state of backsliding

In great pain and regret, Rose, for the first time, read Larry's letter to the end. Days of tearing such a letter before reading it half way were long gone. With sober reflection, Rose gently went through, pondering on the words of her brother. She wished she had received such hot warnings before that time. But it was too late. May be if she had, she could have made up her mind for the Lord again before the trumpet blew and could have been numbered among that happy throng now at the Marriage Supper of the Lamb. Her eyes, for another time, scanned through the skies, oh no, her tear-dimmed eyes could neither see hope nor anything close to it. Rather, they blinked back hot tears of regret on Larry's heart-melting letter. Not long, Rose discovered her misery. All of a sudden, a light was flashed into her being. "You can be redeemed again," thus the Holy Spirit whispered to her. Not long again, she heard; "Seize this last chance!" That was the Holy Spirit calling on Rose the second time. It all appeared to Rose as a mystery. Really it was. However, the mystery may be partly staked on Larry's prayer-soaked letter, because no time had this boy written a salvation piece to anybody, particularly to her erring sister, without going on his knees to wet the letter with prayer, asking the Lord to place His breath on the wordings. As such, the experience of Rose after reading the letter was the work Larry had asked the Holy Spirit to do through the letter before he posted it and before he went away to meet the Lord up yonder.

All that happened to Rose that afternoon took place right in their living room where series of prayer meetings and morning devotions had taken place in the past. Over there on the centre table was a piece of bread, a jar of honey, and somewhere beneath the table laid Roseline's Bible, old and dusty. She never knew when she moved close to the table, picked up the age old book and rubbed her dusty cover on her chest with admiration. She opened to the Book of Revelation and voraciously read some chapters. Her memory came back home. She recollected her once cherished spiritual state before her 'sun' went down. The power of returning to the Lord seemed to be much more present, heaven buoying her spirit. Rose remembered Calvary again and fell on her knees. She sought for restoration through the Saviour. She raised her voice high up to heaven for mercy and forgiveness. The prodigal Rose made it like another prayer meeting of those past days of grace by not being in a hurry. She wired and wired apology to God in the utmost reverence it deserved.

At last, she got up her knees with deep assurance of real salvation experience. Calvary landed her on the safe harbour again. Beaming with joy and singing along one of her old assembly's hymn: *'In tenderness He sought me,'* she headed for Christ Home-going Church; perhaps she would meet anyone to share her experience with.

She increased the volume of her voice with stanza one as she entered the deserted lonely church premises, where nobody worshipped again since the departure of most members and leaders to glory.

In tenderness He sought me,
Weary and sick with sin,
And on His shoulders brought me
Back to His fold again.
While angels in His presence sang,
Until the courts of heaven rang
Oh, the love that sought me!
Oh, the blood that bought me!
Oh, the grace that brought me to the fold,
Wondrous grace that brought me to the fold!

18 - 'MESSIAH' IN DISGUISE

Coveland, a nation affected by the Tribulation mayhem, had a strong concern for her citizenry, particularly, in respect of the disasters and high scale devastation of the time. Obviously, every government, through media agencies, would like to explain to her people the nation's state of affairs whenever the political scene is unsettled or bedevilled by trouble and chaos. This tends to allay fear on the part of the masses and dismiss all available rumours. No doubt, this was the rationale behind the press briefing convened by the Coveland Secretary of State, who had been in attendance at series of meetings organized by the world new government.

At the press briefing, squads of press men and roving photographers in attendance were drawn from different media organizations within the country. With a sense of curiosity, they fielded questions from religious cum political state of the nation at that time. Dr. Taijil, a clear thinking, good-humoured spokesman for Coveland Government, responded to every question in the spirit of fairness. This is the excerpt of the briefing.

Press Briefing by Honourable Kasturi B. Taijil, The Secretary of State, Coveland Government House, Coveland.

Mr. Lewis, State Adviser on Media issues, introduced the Secretary of State:

'The Secretary, as everyone knows, had been in attendance at various conferences convened by the world Administrator since inception. In those conferences, matters affecting peace and foreign policy had been discussed. To inform you about the general state of things at present, gentlemen of the Press and members of the Fourth Estate whose duty is to educate the public, he will begin to provide explanations on the world new government, the state of affairs of the

Republic of Coveland and then take your questions. Now, Honourable Secretary Sir!'

Secretary Taijil: Thank you Mr. Lewis. Really, we have been to series of meetings with the new Administrator. As you all know, the world is now to operate as a single entity in governance and policy, although each nation retains her territorial sovereignty. As such, the representative of each country present at the world summits owes it a duty to keep the members of public informed about the policies and programmes of this seven-year administration. This statement presupposes that your counterparts in other parts of the world shall be gathering like this for the same challenge to which you are here invited. Therefore, you're formally welcome to this briefing, gentlemen of the Press. It is my hope that the media organization which each of you represents will be a good harbinger of my message and all that matter for dissemination in support of the world 'messiah' through your voice, pen and paper (laughter).

Now, as you are all aware, the world was rocked by the most shocking and unusual incident some months ago, when a large sum of people disappeared indefinitely in what was later known as *Rapture*. This ushered in the world single government and this present administration. Since then, I'm sure you will agree with me without protest, that scores of projects which nations statesmen had found difficult to carry out for years have been executed by this administration within a short period of being in office. You can bear me witness that economy no longer nosedives. Or, gentlemen, don't you see that bills no more suffer delay of ratification and promises delay of fulfilment? Or, are we not witnessing issues being attended to with speed? I hope you can recall the reflationary policy of last two months, a promise made good within seventy-two hours with a release of much cash to stimulate the global economy.

With all that, gentlemen and ladies, if you will not call me a sycophant in your press release of tomorrow, I will say this is the best government ever (Y-e-s... all shouted and clapped).

As you must have all learnt by now, our great statesman and political diplomat has emerged to reign with full force like nobody ever before him. He shall be seven years in office. Anyway, you shouldn't wonder too far on why he has seven-year tenure. The reason for that is slated for future discussion.

Let me just talk briefly about few of his political manifestos. I'm sure we all know that the Jewish Temple has been rebuilt. If you can recall, some of you reporters carried that news sometime ago that worship and sacrifices had started again in the Jewish Temple as had been done by their forefathers. That was one of his goals and he has achieved it. For your information and to further confirm that their messiah has indeed, arrived, our man has also entered into a seven-year agreement with Israel. There is evidence also that ten kings from the East and North will make alliance with him and give him unusual support. With all these, a reasonable man will agree that this is the man we need - a man who can telescope action with a policy of peaceful administration.

Once again erudite journalists and media consummates, I must tell you that many plans there are that are yet in the pipe, which this government has for the world and which shall unquestionably unfold in due time. Just keep your fingers crossed and wait for them. I have but little time in my disposal as much as you do. However, let me say that the Republic of Coveland among comity of nations cannot afford to fail in the way we render an unalloyed support to the 'messiah' of our time and, of course, of the world. On your part, use your pen, paper and voice to win him disciples at all cost.

Let me stop for the moment and welcome any questions or queries available for me. Thank you (cheer and ovation burst open from the audience).

Ques: [Sweetlady *F.M*] Mr. Secretary, thanks for that excellent delivery. But what can you say about the close down of Meridian Square?

Ans: Uh-huh... You see, not only Meridian Square is shut down at the moment. All major markets and emporia all over the world are under lock and key for now.

Ques: [Cov.*T.V*] Then, to what extent can you justify this administration as one telescoping action with policy of peace?

Ans: I said the shutdown is a national issue. It has to be taken that way. We can't controvert it at this end. Okay?

Ques: [Newsday] Mr. Secretary, on a related subject, the Apocalyptic Books reveal that His Excellency "through a policy shall also cause craft to prosper and magnify himself in his heart and by peace shall destroy many." Is there any line of reconciliation between that statement and the present mass destruction of lives?

Ans: Yes... yes, you are right. Uh... (Exhibiting some reservation) that is who he is! That statement has a direct reference to the incumbent world leader.

Ques: [County Mag.] Dr. Taijil, earlier in your speech, you referred to the new administrator as "A Messiah." It is the phrase "A messiah" I want to comment on. In all respect, a messiah is expectedly a deliverer and trouble-shooter. How does this apply to the incumbent world leader with this high mortality rate and steaming wars in diverse places?

Ans: (He curled his fingers into fists) Well, as you know, only the very person on the seat of power can answer such question on why he really prefers to be called a messiah in spite of the wars and mass destruction of lives as you have observed. It's difficult for me to interpret such paradox.

Ques: [Cov.Times] Where really will be the seat of the new government?

Ans: Simply Babylon for now! But in the middle of his reign, Jerusalem.

Ques: [The Mark] Mr. Secretary, based on the fundamental belief of the Christian doctrine, do you anticipate a future disagreement or friction between Israel and the present government?

Ans: Without being a prophet of doom, I mean to be frank, we expect not only disagreement but war towards the middle of his reign.

Ques: [Newsday] Dr. Taijil, if I could take you back to the Holy Writ again, please pardon me, it is on record that the world leader will turn a dictator eventually. Not only that, he will force men to take certain mark, 666, if I'm correct, and whoever rejects the mark will be mercilessly killed. Are you in agreement with such prediction?

Ans: (He gasped with relief) well, for now such has not been declared by him but the Holy Writ is true! And we know it would be as it is said. He will force men to do so.

Ques: [Sweetlady *F.M*] Do you have the timetable of his tenure, particularly when such mark may likely be introduced?

Ans: Gentlemen, I am not in position to tell you the time. However, to be fair to you and to the best of my knowledge, the introduction of the mark will be around the middle of his seven-year administration.

Ques: [Cov.Times) The Secretary, what shall be the structure of his government and who are in his cabinet.
Ans: Well, as to the structure of his government, he has many parts to that. We have to wait and see. But besides one certain prophet who shall champion his programme, we know also that no less than ten kings will give him their power and the prince of this world will give him his power also.

Ques: [Newsday] Sir, what would you have to tell our people at home about Armageddon?

Ans: As for the Battle of Armageddon, it is meant to come as the climax of this on-going seven-year reign. It shall be fierce, severe and brutal.

Ques:[Sweetlady F.M] Sir, are you aware too that the battle will be between the Son of the Most High God (who is coming with his raptured saints soon) and the armies of His opposers: the Dragon, the Beast and the False Prophet?
Ans: You are correct; after the battle comes the reign of peace of one thousand years of the great King.

"With this, gentlemen and ladies, I shall draw a curtain on today's press briefing. It has been an exciting time having you here. You people are doing great job for the nation. I hope when next we have a need of your attention, you wouldn't disappoint us. Many thanks and have a nice day."

19 - THE FLASHBACK

The strains from the keyboard were soft and sweet. The florid decoration on the altar shed a romantic glow as Florence moved slowly down the aisle in her flowing white satin gown sewn by the best bridal shop in the City, with the Chief bride maid behind. Hundred of eyes began to cast glances at her and at her flower-decorated hand as she moved ahead in such an elegant way that sincerely gave the invitees and well-wishers in attendance a thrilled impulse of conjugal bliss. She soon joined the handsome bridegroom, Pauli, already seated in front of the altar, waiting to be accompanied by the 'queen'. Not long, the occasion kicked off proper. "I do" blared along at the hearing of the guests as one of the left-behind pastors conducted the wedding between Florence and Pauli in Coveland City.

This account, a reader should not forget, was a flashback of the marriage ceremony of Florence and Dave Pauli which came up well over two years ago, precisely four weeks after the Rapture of the saints.

At any rate, wedding scene is always lovely. It can be sweet in the connotative use of word; however, not for all couples. Not for Pauli and Florence either, where the former had deflowered the latter before their marriage and a three-month pregnancy had been aborted before the conjugal knot was tied - the singular act that robbed them of their fitness for the glorious Rapture of the saints. Little wonder, cheerfulness was a difficult task for the duo on their wedding day and confusion made companionship of them. That was why in spite of all the pomp, glitz and glamour that friends and relation invited tried to inject into the ceremony, smiling was alien to their faces, the guilt and wound of the crime being fresh in their memory. They did know, of course, that their home had been built on gun-powder. Pauli and Florence did not heed the warning of the Bible as it affects the holy wedding. Probably when they ought to have kept a gap, love excitement did not allow them to see the danger ahead or perhaps they kidded each other into thinking that premarital sexual compatibility was the hallmark of a successful union. Here they were in the City of Coveland, left behind to share in the portion of the ugly and painful era of the Antichrist.

As the year rolled by, time brought changes to Coveland City. Events upon events had come and gone, and series of catastrophic occurrences had been caused in diverse places just in line with the prophecy of the Holy Bible recorded in Revelation chapter six verses 1-8. And for the sake of their faith and heaven, many of those people who had settled with God in the early period of those terrible days had been killed too, all in compliance with the prophecy of the Holy Writ contained in Revelation Chapter 6 verses 9-11.

Other natural cataclysms had also been recorded. At least, meteors were reported falling in some parts of the city; earthquake, sun turning black and moon becoming red as blood were the experiences of the people on the earth at that time, mostly in Mediterranean and European regions (Rev. 6:12-17).

Soon, like in a twinkle of an eye, the new government clocked three years and six months in office. As if he had been waiting for that, the Antichrist broke his former agreement with Israel and destroyed the religious system mentioned thousands years ago by Prophet Daniel (Dan. 9:27), which Apostle John also saw in his vision (Rev. 17:16-18). This world 'diplomat', as journalists that time were fond of calling him, was soon on his way to reign in Jerusalem and sit in the temple of God where abomination of desolation will be placed to confirm so many Scriptures (Dan.9:27; 11:45; 2Thess. 2:4). However, all the while he had been crusading himself as a great one and the messiah of the Jews.

One day, certain circular, or rather an edict was passed round hospitals and medical centres by the Coveland Health Authority. It bore the '666' seal, Antichrist being referred to within its content as 'His Excellency'. Before the week of issue ran out, it had found its way to the notice board and walls of hospital wards so that patients and relations could read for themselves and address their minds to the new policy being advocated.

The circular, though short, two paragraphs in all, was authoritative and unsparing. Besides its unusual heading of '**No 666, No Medication**' in bold type, it couched its last statement as follows: "**In the interest of everyone who needs medical attention, either as in-**

patient or out-patient, citizen or foreigner, obtainment of '666' mark of the Beast is a must."

The Paulis had their second child, Theophilus, at Coveland General Hospital around that time. Theo was born a premature. As such, it was being nursed in an incubator to keep it warm and was being fed by means of medicine dropper. Coveland General Hospital, one of the preferred hospitals of the time, received a copy of the said circular that week and treated it with noblest regard. Pronto, it had sent copies round all the departments; in fact, it was a copy per ward. In no time at all, a copy had found its way to ward 8 where Florence was.

"Theo is improving, Madam. I am just from Special Care Unit now", Nurse Jones who was on morning duty cosily commented about Theophilus.

"Thank you nurse, only I don't find this engorgement all that easy," Florence replied.

"Uh…you see, you have to endure it for the moment. By the time you start breastfeeding him directly, you'll have a relief."

"Would Dr. Olivia be around for morning ward-round today?"

"You'll like to see her?"

"Yes."

"I don't know. But she should. At least, she was here yesterday. But have you read the circular pasted on the wall at the corridor?"

"Circular? What is it all about?"

"It's called **'No 666, No Medication'**."

"No 666, No Medication? I haven't."

"You better go and read it because from 12.00 noon today, doctors will no longer be attending to patients who have no '666' on either palms or foreheads."

"What are you talking about, nurse? '666' is too serious to joke with!" Florence responded in a low tone with her eyes beaming warning.

"I don't know, Madam. All I know is that there is a '666' embargo on medical treatment."

"No, nurse, not just yet! I reject that," Florence shouted.

"Please, don't implicate me. If you're not convinced, go to the notice board yourself," she whizzed off.

Florence jumped out of her ward with some trepidation. Surprise weighed her down when she saw how the long sprawling corridor of the hospital block was dotted with people in threes and fours standing in awe with eyes glued to the walls of their wards. Lifting up her head right there in the hospital corridor, Florence clapped eyes on a copy of the circular already pasted near the entrance door of ward 8 where she was. In eerie silence, she read and re-read, tracing and retracing with fingers the statements in bold type. At first, she was dumbfounded and motionless as she recalled series of her Pastor's preaching upon preaching on '666' Mark of the Antichrist and the aftermath of receiving it.

What does someone expect from a person who had been warned and had likewise warned others against the same incident? Hardly had Florence reached the last line of the notice before she broke into a shivery sob. As if scourged by November sun, she began to perspire profusely. Sweat drenched her clothes. After that scene of reality, she went in; sat down and called back to mind how life had been since she fell from glory and grace. Everything played itself backward as if a tape. Right inside the ward, she began to cry unto God. It was evident to Florence that the time to decide for one's eternal end by one's own blood or eternal doom by taking the mark of the Beast had dawned. At the same time, thought about what might become of Theophilus should the baby be denied of Medicare just for a day, began to cluster around her heart.

20 - '666' OF THE ANTICHRIST

It was quite enigmatic the way the whole world, not only Coveland City, had changed within few days after the false prophet, that flattering sycophant, introduced the Mark of the Antichrist; the introduction which let loose tension and terror upon the world. A few days later, it was as if ages upon ages had rolled by the way crises and mayhem had crippled the order of things in a typical country as Coveland.

To worsen it, the Antichrist himself, that evil genius, tactician, usurper and wicked son of perdition, had declared himself as God in a national telecast. Not long, '666' became a maxim; a mark to be taken without a room for a rethink, where collection was subject to no exception. In human history, no mark had carried so forceful a demand of acceptance as that of the Antichrist, neither had there ever been a man in history who had so defrauded the public of their revered freedom of choice like this pseudo-peaceful dictator, not Idiamin of Uganda, not Benito Mussolini, not even Antiochus Epiphany, nor Herod, nor General Titus even in the destruction of Jerusalem in A.D 70. Antichrist, a man to be feared for the power he wielded and the draconian law he used; a dictatorial administrator, so notorious for inhuman jailing and heartless killing. So upsetting as a bridgeless river was the era of the Beast government [2Thess.3:2-10], where peace was rank shifted to a Lilliput and frustration was grown to an oak tree for tallness. In those days who dare oppose him? Or who had guts to read any disability to the edicts of the man of sin. As such, human whims and fancy became increasingly restrictive, adding more a burden to their struggle for survival.

That was how the Beast's Mark, '666', became institutionalized all over the nations. In Coveland, for instance, several centres in form of polling booths were opened as collection centres. Just to mention a few, one centre was conspicuously cited at G.R.A for the resident civil servants. Another centre was along Venus Boulevard towards the government villa, mainly for the Number one Citizen and his retinue of personal assistants, security agents, cooks and messengers. Within Marine Polytechnic, there were two centres. And for its population, the University of Coveland alone had five centres within her main campus.

Within a short time, many had collected the mark. Some preferred it on their foreheads; others had it stamped behind their palms. Once the mark was received, no more hope of being saved forever. The receiver became ultimately and eternally alienated from anything called grace. He sealed his doom whoever had it! From experience, at least from the way Lynda and Chum, her husband, a newspaper vendor, reacted shortly after sealing their doom by taking the mark, it was obvious that the Beast's wicked mark of '666' made people more or less demon-like in emotion, thought and character. Because as soon as the couple took the mark, they became kind to oppression and were especially thirsty of blood. A receiver of the Antichrist's Mark would act as if he had swallowed the content in Satan's goblet of wickedness to the dreg. Blasphemy against the Almighty God became a song for such. Recipients paid no heed to human crying; blinkers had covered their eyes of mercy.

Because his coming was after the working of Satan with all power, signs and lying wonders, Antichrist, within a short while, had exerted a vast network of influence over human minds and decisions. Before anybody knew it, he had circumscribed the minds of the most active segment of the population of Coveland - the Coveland University Students. They had started collecting the mark with speed without question. The same trend that ran through the students soon connected their lecturers. Overnight, their critical minds were won over. Many of those lecturers could not just go against the draconian laws of the dictator. He had really worked on them that they never remembered to bring his regime to book through any of their criticism courses and ideological theories by which they had 'crucified' past governments that ruled in tyranny and commended rulers that reigned with transparency.

To extend massive expansion within a limited time, the Antichrist's government quickly embarked on recruiting young people into the Beast Army as officers and posting them to local councils and district areas. These were meticulously done and, of course, in a haste. Small wonder, every circular passed to'666' collection centres often borne this terse mission statement: *'So short the time; so much the work.'* The officers were unflagging optimists, dedicated miscreants, committed, meticulous and dead serious sycophants. As for appearance, their uniforms tallied with one of the military. On their black trousers was a broad red stripe of the general staff and their tunics were decorated on the right and left sleeves with the number, 666, in red colour as their insignia of office. Their countenance was always obsessed by wickedness to its sophistication. Without debate, it was only someone who had seen an owl in his life that could describe how the eyes of these officers had 'vacated' the right place in the socket, bulging out as if to fall away at any moment.

Often times, when a Christian who could not endure that grinding hunger came around for the mark, rather than reeling out those owl-like eyes, the officers would meet him with a huge dreamy smile. If such person appeared to be somehow hesitant, probably he remembered that taking the mark amounted to signing of one's doom; they would warm up his brain a bit with sweet words. If their trick won, the demon-indwelling officers would shoot appreciative glances at the man. However, if such refused to allow himself to be treated a small fry or an utter fool or, perhaps, a bastard nonentity concluding not to take the mark, they would arrest him as a religious dissident. It was from there he would be made to cross over to the Old June Prison which had cells that looked so tiny and smelt damp, with barely enough space for fresh air.

At Coveland during the time in question, homes were not better for those Christians who got restored after the Rapture and those who newly discovered the way of light. Campuses were worse. Students who later reconciled with the Lord at that time were passing through an excruciating experience. No lecturer would register any student for his course unless such student presented the Beast's Mark. Taxi drivers, besides their fares, would demand 666 ID. Supermarket was not different. Neither was canteen ready to sell food to any customer that didn't have it. The public was on its peak of brutalities. Jailing and killing persisted on non-possessors of the mark of the Antichrist. How unfortunate to remain here during the time!

21 - DAVE'S DILLEMA

Soon after the Rapture occurrence of those years, Pastor Ray Fred of the defunct Daily Shower Interdenominational became aware of how misleading his preaching had been to his congregation with the whole of 96% left behind. With a deep sense of regret, he closed down his "Shower Interdenominational" as fondly called, and called on God for his own salvation. Ray Fred did confess to those church members of his to whom instrumental he was of missing that glorious Rapture, that he had been a blind man trying to lead the blind by setting up that wear-what-you-want and do-as-you-like gospel centre. Ray dropped his prophecy enterprise for a Wesleyan model of gospel campaign begging and pleading with his left-behind church members to repent by all means. Before Antichrist's open declaration of himself as God, Ray had set up a secret place of meeting at Meadow County in Coveland, where he committed himself to encouraging people to come back to God after he had seen the truth of the Scripture in the light of the events around. He enlightened them that the Millennial Reign of the Lord would soon roll in and, as such, they should settle with the Lord and hold fast to their faith even before the Antichrist. However, Ray could only win just few to the safe harbour. The pressure of suffering of those years was too unbearable for so many people and the night of grieving seemed too long and painful. Even many of his own former wear-what-you-want church members could not wait any longer for the new light Ray was trying to light. Unbelievably, many of the scattered 'Daily Showers' members subscribed to taking the mark even after they had been told of the consequence of doing that. How terrible! Who truly can endure these, surviving that agony to receiving the crown?

At the moment, Roseline Abdullah had joined Meadow County secret church. Janet's parents, Mr. and Mrs. Frank equally were members. Not long, a number of people who had heard about the danger of the '666' Mark of the Beast soon joined them. Bible used to be hidden away inside a bag or newspaper when coming for meeting. No microphone or loudspeaker; no praise worship, of course, no music in this underground gathering. As days went by, the decision of the time began to move from general to particular. For example in Dave Pauli's office, a time came when it became mandatory for workers to show their '666' Mark before collecting their wages. At first, only junior workers were affected, but later, it was extended to the senior staff. The only excuse given in this respect by the management was that the instruction had come from the head office.

Remember, Theophilus had been born as premature and had since been hospitalized at Coveland

General Hospital. When no treatment was forthcoming because Florence, his mother, had refused to take the mark and doctors would not attend to babies whose parents had no '666', Theophilus had been seriously ill. For your information, a week and two days later after Theophilus fell sick, he died! Oh, you're surprised? Not only you, I too cast a vote of sympathy in this end. On his own, Nathan, the first child of this couple, who was in primary two, had been asked to stay away from school until his parents showed up. Why? You asked? What was obtainable in the Primary school then was that both parents must appear in their child's school with the mark of the Beast on their foreheads or in their palm before their child would be allowed into the classroom. All these mounted unbearable pressure on Dave, a man who had not properly regained a good spiritual template and divine stamina since his terrible fall into fornication before the wedding. A man whose problem became compounded by his loss of making the Rapture, Dave had no inner fibre enough to carry through.

"Our baby has died; Nathan has been ejected from school; salary is not paid all because of '666', why die in hunger? I'll better accept the mark" Dave reasoned.

For days, Florence had been staying indoors waiting patiently for her death. No food. It was three days ago since they ate food in that house. Nathan was lean, tired of crying. Nobody could predict what may likely happen to that boy if care is not taken. Meanwhile, Florence no more had money in her bank account due to Theophilus' illness. If she had at all, she would not have access to just a penny until she has shown her '666' identity on the counter.

"My dear, we knew of this before this time. It is only a pity that we are victims of it in the long run. Let's die inside our predicament and be part of Tribulation

Saints than going out for food and fall into the hands of the oppressor," Florence counseled.

"Die here? Where is death since all these days? This is the third day since we ate in this house. We've been waiting and death has not found us to kill? Let me collect the mark to save this home though I'll be lost forever," Dave declared.

"Dear, no, never! You're not taking that terrible mark...," Florence declared kneeling down and pleading with Dave in tears.

"Flore... stand up. Just stand up. You see, Theo has gone; I can't allow Nathan also to die in my presence. I rather collect the mark than having no seed behind. If no help comes before evening, I would dam the consequence. Be informed!" Dave frankly disclosed.

"Dear, please, if that be the case, let me go to a friend nearby if she could help us with some food items. But the mark is not the solution, I beg..."

"Don't be late!"

Oppression makes a man mad. Dave Pauli's case was a typical example. Hunger had gnawed his conviction to insignificance. If he had had the knowledge of being left behind, he would have given Rapture all the watchfulness it demanded. But he was now witnessing the era of that snake-handling dictator and hysterical demagogue — the Antichrist, as he liked to be called. What would Dave do? He appeared like a man hearing two different tunes, who, no doubt, has the problem of which one to dance to. The way things are now, who can tell whether Dave would not take the mark? While on one side the danger signal was blinking too fast, on the other side Dave had staked his decision on one of the uncertainties of the time — food. Should Dave receive the mark, it means all is gone. It means all hope is lost. He will not reach the City beyond the river, where the saints will sing angelic songs so melodious 'forever in the sweet by and by'. Should Dave make a mistake of accepting '666' regardless of how grinding the hunger and ferocious the time, when at the set of sun, in mansion beyond the blue, when saints of God are in joy unspeakable, tears of ever once being a Christian but lost in transit would forever make companionship of his eyes.

We pray he doesn't fall, but what happened later is in some chapters ahead.

22 - THE CAPTURE

As we know temple to be one of the glories of ancient Greece and amphitheatre her glory of art, so did Coveland citizens know desolation so much as to be a household word during the Great Tribulation. The devastation was much. It was a city long past its glory days; it had been wasted beyond description. Christians who had no '666' found it tough to move about. It was a great risk to do so. You dare not carry Bible openly because the Antichrist's regime recognized whoever proclaimed that Jesus is Lord as a rebel. That was why several church buildings had been burnt down. Imagine, if ordinarily the 'Christianity' of jazz and pop music and one well spiced with mini skirt and all Hollywood belongings no longer found a place to swirl in a bubbling stew as before, what then do we expect would become of anyone who said holiness is real or that the Antichrist was an impostor? How hard to make it during the period; how foolish to disdain the advantage now!

Back to Florence' story, by and large, she found favour with her friend. She was fed to satisfaction. Being so kind, her friend sent her away with some food items that could sustain them for, at least, a week. Immediately, Florence began to come back. She would not delay on the way to prevent her family from dying of hunger or going for the terrible mark as her husband had said.

Unknown to Florence – unlucky Florence, permit me to say that – six of the Beast force men with their wagon were on raiding trip to her area. They were somewhere at the street corner where she would pass. Because the thought of being at home was glowing fondly in her memory, her trekking had inadvertently increased. This brisk movement had allowed the Beast's men to take notice of her amid some passers-by.

"E-e-esh woman, stop there," in a gruff voice, one of the stout men who held a whip in his right hand and was busy jangling handcuff in the left with the most wicked countenance ever, ordered Florence to stop.

"Me?" Florence asked, pointing to herself.

"Yes, you! What do you carry?"

"Food items sir."

"From where to where?"

"From a friend's place."

"Can you identify yourself?"

"I'm sorry; I'm not here with my I.D card!"

"Which I.D card? I said you should show me your '666' Mark."

"I'm a civil servant, officer."

"Yes, civil servants like other citizens have no immunity from receiving the mark."

"I have no such a mark."

"You don't have wh-a-t" his eyes flashed anger.

"I'm sorry sir."

"Okay, I'm giving you the mark here now. By now you should have got it if you really wanted to."

"'666'? Not me."

"Not you? Are you a Christian?" His anger burnt as a furnace again.

"I am," immediately, ridges of cold sweat began to gather on Florence' brows as she boldly replied this 'monster'.

"Ohoo! You're now talking. So, Christianity has made you a lawless citizen? In the name of the Beast, you're taking the mark today..."

"Never. In the name of Jesus, I reject the mark of the Beast..."

Nothing infuriated this puffy red-eyed man than this. Before Florence knew it, she had been dumped inside the wagon by one of the other five men. That was how Florence was taken to Old June Prison Camp, where

Christians in Coveland who rejected the Beast's mark were being gruesomely tortured. If anyone remained tenacious to his decision, he would be burnt, beheaded, boiled in hot water, fried in hot oil, electrocuted or released to a poisonous reptile to eat. Or, at worst, be butchered like a ram. However, none of these could overthrow heaven from the heart of the determined, imperturbable, only-by-death-quenchable Florence.

While yet inside the wagon, Florence experienced an abrupt rush of home sickness. She remembered her husband and Nathan her son. While praying and occasionally peeping through the window as the Beast's officer stopped over and again to carry out raids on those having no '666', she suddenly saw in the crowd a man who lived on the same street with her. She beckoned on him to move nearer. In two sentences, Florence sent home a message and the major part of the food items.

23 - BY THEIR OWN BLOOD

As for the Old June Prison Camp, it was built and monitored in the way that showed that all the Beast's regime was after was just the number of souls that could renounce the Lordship of Christ for '666' - the mark of doom - rather than the number of those being brutally killed. We cannot question this given the way many public places had instantly turned to veritable hide-outs for the Beast's officers to carry out massive raids on non-possessors of the mark, with pressure to obtain it either by hook or by crook. I thought it idyllic to let you know the way these cells were built on twenty acres of land. As for location, to start with, the Old June Prison Camp was easy to reach. No Taxi driver in Coveland would tell you he does not understanding what you mean just at the mention of the name. This is because the Old June Camp was the next place to reach immediately after the uncompleted Coveland National Stadium. All you need do is just to wave down a taxi cab; you will be surprised you are at the Camp with a ten-minute drive, especially if you take off from any of her metropolitan districts. Most drivers liked to take Council Road, others liked Justice Avenue. The former was shorter. One old big iron gate is the first thing to inform you that you are already in front of the jail with the name boldly written on it in horizontal form.

The whole premises were sandy as if it were a sea side or, if you like, call it bar beach. Over thirty blocks of buildings lined up in an arc shape from the left down to the right of the bloody land. Each block has a corridor and ten cells. Each cell was designed for three prisoners. You can imagine the smallness of the prison home, a 'kitchenette' to put it in a mild way. The blocks were arranged in order of Block 1 cell A, B, C..., Block 2 cell A, B, C... and so on and so forth. In the front of each block, about a pole away, were three stakes. To these were

Christians being tied and brutally set ablaze on daily basis as many as rejected the mark of the Beast. Somewhere at the centre of the premises was a place we could call a roundabout. Just at the middle over there was a flag raised - a rebel flag that displayed the picture of the Antichrist.

Friend, to cut the long story short, this was the place Florence found herself on that bitterest evening. Usually, the first thing the Raiding Unit would do on arrival from each trip was to match those tenacious Christians fondly called 'prisoners of war' for ridicule to an officer at the Registration Unit who would take down their names, residential addresses and, as well, allocate them cells.

Florence with the rest others was matched to the Registration Unit. The officer in charge took down her particulars before handling her to the officer in charge of Block 6.

"Florence or what did you say your name is?" the Registration Officer asked.

"Florence..." she answered.

"Follow that man. Offic...er," he shouted.

"S...ir."

"Put her in cell "B" Block 6. But woman, hear this before you go, never you think there is a way of escape for you unless you produce your '666' Mark. If you like yourself, you better collect it before capital punishment will deny you opportunity to do so. That is my advice. Go!"

So, Florence was taken to Block 6 cell 'B' where she met the greatest surprise of her life.

Mercy Oke used to be a student of Hero Grammar School till her arrest by the Beast's officers. While in elementary school, Mercy was a good, serious and religious pupil. Florence had contributed appreciably to

Mercy's good moral behaviour having being a teacher in the school that time. While there, Florence loved to teach pupils morals in the morning devotion by telling stories of Joseph the dreamer, Samuel the well-behaved and Daniel the uncompromising.

No sooner had Mercy finished her elementary school and gained admission to Hero Grammar School than she got hooked by peer group's whim and fancy. Meanwhile, before then, 'Hero Gram.' as her school was called for short, used to be a reputable school all parents wanted their children to attend. The standard was superb. The certificate results of the out-going students used to be next to impeccable, the talk of the town. Mention it, Hero Gram was always ahead in everything. Unfortunately the most difficult thing in life is not to set a standard, but to maintain it. At the time Mercy joined the school, Hero was no longer hero in the real sense of the term. Her light had gone into obscurity and what constituted the standard it was notable for had ebbed away like sand at the seashore. You know, it is common for human beings to live in the past glory. That was exactly the case with Hero Grammar School. It was still dancing in the old costume, although it had cases of sexual promiscuity among girls in upper classes and some male teachers, beside series of examination leakages to show for her downward slope in both moral and academic standard. Many students could not avoid playing on this slanting 'chessboard'. They could not beat the tumbling social vices at Hero. Even Mercy herself who appeared chaste and serious could not, though religious.

However, when the Rapture took place and the Antichrist came on board as the World Diplomat, Mercy remembered perfectly well that when she was in primary five Aunty Florence had spoken about this man. She recollected that in a morning devotion one day, a long pictorial chart in the form of a scroll containing the pictures of the Antichrist and the False Prophet was brought by their Aunty to teach the pupils the evil of '666' to be introduced when godly children would have gone with Jesus. Mercy remembered quite vividly how Aunty Florence had said the mark of this diabolic would be forced on the young and old who would miss the Lord's return at Rapture. Not only that but how anybody who collected it would be eternally doomed. Though that was many years ago, yet it remained green in her memory as if it were said the previous day. With all these, Mercy Oke now made up her mind never to take the Antichrist's mark even if she would be punished for it. This girl met her ordeal in one of those days when Beast's Force Men were invading schools about. How did it happen?

A day prior to the incident, Mercy had informed her classmates all that the mark involved and how they should cooperate to reject it whenever the givers visited their school. Everybody consented! As if it were a prophecy, in the following morning, the '666' agents touched down at Hero College to give students the mark. What do you expect from a band of ignorant students? They quickly formed single files in front of their classrooms waiting for their doom. A whole lot of these students thought it was a means of winning admission to study in Universities abroad. This much the more made some of them rushed out while others jumped the line collecting their 'obituaries' with speed. It is a pity! The exercise was rapid. Not long it reached Mercy's class, but the students objected. Or, let us say they protested. When force was employed, they raised alarm shouting 'No! No, we're not taking. It is satanic! It is *antigod*! It is Antichrist's!' I tell you, it was a serious uproar that morning. This issue we are talking about shook Hero. It took the school authorities a lot of efforts to calm down the aggrieved few. When investigation was made later on, it was discovered that Mercy Oke was the brain behind the rampage. Before the power that be, Mercy was a dissident and she had to face the music. So, that was how she met her woe as the Force men took her away to the Old June Prison Camp to explain herself.

Since Mercy came she had been kept inside cell 6 Block 'B'. She had seen a lot and heard a lot. She was being threatened on daily basis to collect the mark or else she would not be released to go home. The promotional examination was approaching, her principal and parents had sent to her to collect the mark and obtain her release, but she was not ready to dance to their tune. It can be surprising at times that whatever is 'planted' in the minds of children in form of dos or don'ts could turn out to become their philosophy of life.

This is the eleventh day since Mercy was arrested and brought into this cell. In spite of the severe hunger, her decision was still like a cobblestone for hardness. She had been told that her offence was Libel, which, according to them, was punishable by death. There was nothing anybody could do about it unless she withdrew her statement and confessed that Antichrist was the Messiah and not Jesus before she could be set acquitted. But in so far as Mercy had remained adamant and was never ready to be persuaded to change what had been driven into her mind long ago, she would pay dearly for it.

It had been like a child's play all along not until the officer in charge of cells in Block 6 passed a circular to the inmates of the ten cells in that block, even to Mercy, that at 10.00am the following day, Mercy Oke in Rm 'B' would be greeting the land of the living a final farewell on stake 2 in front of their block. So, everybody else should be ready as if to say 'dust for dust and ash for ash' to Mercy. Since morning when Mercy received the circular, she had been sick and perplexed. Her eyes were red and swollen. Different thoughts had engaged her mind; one thought coming after the other in such a rapid succession that hardly gave her enough time to think through. At 3.00pm that same day, the officer in charge called back with another brand of persuasion.

"Since you came here Mercy", the officer disclosed, "you're a witness to it that no fewer than thirty people have died by boiling, frying and burning. You could have been one of them, but I have kept on promising the Executioner Unit to be patient and allow you to have a rethink and make a wise choice, not forgetting that you're a teen. I made them realize that it takes a long time for the young people to think through before they make up their minds. This is what has delay the verdict to this time. But at this point, I want to let you know that I have tried all within my disposal. Since you insist that the ruler is no Messiah and '666' is satanic, never to be collected by you, it has now been concluded that you should be tied to the stake tomorrow, just as you must have read in the circular passed around in the morning, and be burnt! Period. However, it is not late yet. If you can take your time to think through before the evening and be ready to drop your faith, you can let me know. I can still help prepare your paper overnight together with others' decision extracts to be submitted tomorrow, so that your release can be first thing tomorrow morning."

This heart-melting demon-coated speech almost made Mercy change her mind immediately. But her reply as usual was not more than a sentence: 'I have heard!' That was what she said and the officer went away.

In fear and trembling, Mercy began to count minutes and hours as they were passing by. At last, she made up her mind that whenever the man entered her cell again, she was going to ask him for just one more day of grace to think out something positive.

It was amid this swirling and twisting of thought that Florence, her elementary school teacher, was brought in. What a mystery! Immediately Florence entered the cell, the officer who brought her closed the door behind and went his way.

24 - ULTIMATE CHOICE

Words will fail any attempt to describe the measure of surprise that engaged the prison room the moment Florence and Mercy clapped eyes on each other. It was historic. Mind had series of episodes to recall. Memory had a need to run anticlockwise: flashback upon flashback; anecdote upon anecdote; series of 'do you remember?' and scores of 'yes, I do'. For that moment, at least, they both forgot it was Antichrist's time and that they were in his prison yard. In fact, it was more of mother-child relationship than teacher-student affair. Mercy took time to narrate many of what had happened to her on the rough road to adolescence: several curves, many bends, many bumps till she dragged her story to the event that led to her arrest. She could not help it. She betrayed emotion and cried bitterly.

Florence drew Mercy nearer and mopped her cheeks of those tumbling drops of tears. She offered

Mercy words of comfort and gave her the little food that remained from those given by her friend. No doubt, Mercy showed her teacher the death warrant and what she had decided to do about it. Florence Pauli felt greatly concerned especially when Mercy demanded her for choice most appropriate to take. Really, a dilemma was on ground. A dilemma of which choice was better for this endangered species. Obviously, it was not easy to say go and die; it was equally hard to send her to doom just by saying go for '666'. Yet Mercy must have to cast her vote for either of the two options. Florence too did know that only Mercy could choose which way. But then she had to make the right choice. That is why Florence attended her question in the following words:

"Mercy, all you've said has really proved that this, indeed, is a time of Jacob's trouble, which the Bible talks about. A decision has landed you here and a decision will carry you through the rest rough water of life that remains ahead of you. However, you haven't told me about your conversion experience. Are you redeemed from your sin by the blood?"

"Ma, I don't understand what that means."

"I'm asking whether you have ever confessed your sins to God in prayer and from your heart have turned away from them."

"No!"

"Really?"

"Yes Ma."

"Alright, my dear, that is the decision needed to make you sail through. Quick! Quick! You have to be redeemed. Once that is done, you'll know what choice is better for tomorrow. You're born a sinner like any other human being. Only confession of sin, turning away from the same and faith in Christ as your Lord and Saviour make you a child of God. It gives you access to heaven and to all rights of a heavenly citizen. Angel of death has no power over a truly redeemed soul even at death. You'll have everlasting mansion over there in the company of innumerable saints gone beyond..."

Florence had hardly made an end of speech when Mercy fell into conviction. She began to pray her way through to redemption right in that cell. Heaven recognized her contrite spirit and offered her the needed pardon. After the prayer, they lay their heads on their laps and slept off.

Though sorrow tarries long in the night, joy comes in the morning. This is a true verse we are all quite familiar with. At any rate, for Mercy, events surrounding the latest development seemed not to favour this old age utterance. Because the next morning broke with an angry fist dishing punches of knocks on the prison door repeatedly.

"Praying or sleeping?" the officer roared outside. When he had opened the door, he demanded:

"Mercy, have you now resolved that Jesus is an impostor and not a Messiah, but the Beast is?"

"Never. From here till eternity my Jesus remains the Messiah, Lord and Saviour. The King of ki..." P-a-a-a, a dirty slap that could root out the tooth from its foundation was deposited at Mercy's cheek by this officer to put an end to her declaration of faith. He banged the door and roared away in anger like a dog that sustained an injury by a strayed bullet. Mercy smiled, though in pain of the sudden punch. She praised the Lord as well. Florence, who watched the scenario, observed that of a truth Mercy Oke had really been converted and ready for her home above. From that moment she began to spend time with Mercy in prayer and counselling. She assured her of angels waiting to robe her in fine linen and carry her away to God's mansion.

25 - THE LAST MILE

Sixty minutes to the zero hour, the officer surfaced again. This time, it was not for whether Mercy still believed in Jesus or was ready to believe in the Beast either. Rather, he was around to inform her that at 10.am she would be no more. Mercy's response was 'okay'. Astounded, the officer shook his head not being able to recall when last he handled a human being of this breed. How let down he felt!

That morning, five people were on the execution list. Mercy was the youngest. Thirty minutes to the time, the whole Camp was quiet and the premises wore loneliness as a garment. Movement was restricted. Only executioner officers should be seen in the open place. As the moment drew close, Mercy and Florence knew the time of temporary separation had come. They sang one of the old gospel hymns to greet each other bye-bye for now. After that song, they hugged each other and wept.

Just about ten minute to 10.00am, the prison was opened and Mercy was taken out to confront her death. This is how Mercy Oke was matched out to the stake in front of Block 6. While preparation was in progress, she continued to recite within her: "Death, where is thy power; grave, where is thy victory...Glory to God who gave us victory through our Lord Jesus." Other Christians awaiting their own verdicts were peeping through the smallish windows; Florence was busy praying to God for Mercy to have courage to remain faithful to the end. Everybody kept wondering about Mercy; a young girl of thirteen, clinging to her stake bravely. The Senior Executioner Officer too could not believe his eyes. He descended from his rostrum where he was standing ready to send forth the last order.

"Young girl, why are you here?"

"I'm here to give expression to what I'm convinced is the only way."

"What is the only way?" the officer asked.

"The Cross," Mercy replied.

"Are your parents alive?"

"Yes."

"Have they taken their own marks?"

"I don't know."

"Simply give us your address and let's have them fetched down to replace you. As for you, I can see that future is bright and holds much for you."

"Officer, capital no! As for bright future, you're correct, but not here. It is in my home above. In my Father's house, there are many mansions there."

After so long a persuasion which yielded no fruit, he left the girl alone. At quarter past 10.00am, they had all been well tied to their stakes. The order went out. Fire was set on them. It was not an easy road. The hungry flame coiled around them with its craving 'tongue'. As they toiled in the hand of death, they were busy saying repeatedly 'Jesus you're my Lord and King, not the Antichrist.' Within a short moment, they had been snatched of their skin. In no time at all, their frames had begun to fall apart, turning to ashes gradually. Mercy's skeletal makeup dropped one after the other. Her skull soon fell off its neck. It was a gory sight.

Florence wept. She groaned when in her very face, Mercy's bones began to turn to ashes. She went on her knees and with tears on her cheek, began to sing:

O brother, life's journey beginning,
With courage and firmness arise!
Look well to the course thou art   choosing;
Be earnest, be watchful, and wise!
Remember – two paths are before thee,
And both thy attention   invite;
But one leadeth on to destruction.
The other to joy and delight.

God help you to follow his banner
And serve Him wherever you go;
And when you are tempted, my brother,
God give you the grace to say "No!"

26 - A DISAPPOINTED APPEAL

Belief and opinion are like a zone that is endangered by the angry wind of life. Either of them forms the pedestal on which we stand when our road is rough. When it comes to the declaration of our belief or opinion, evidence has justified it to a sufficient degree that it is at such a time we tend to know more of ourselves, how close or far we stand to God.

However, it would be necessary to say from the outset that belief and opinion are themselves two issues accounting for two different premises. That is to say, the two are by no means the same, though they are 'trees' of the same forest. Some may call them a coin. Good! But, a coin with different faces.

As for opinion, most of its makers, especially those who have substance to show for it, would never want to know whose ox is gored when the challenge of life summons them to give expression to their opinion.

For their adherence to it, they would hardly allow any compromise or disability to emerge from their end. Most often, this is not the case with belief. Most people, who claim to hold one belief or another, more often than not, drop their conviction about such belief by the roadside, their excuse often being attributed to either the trial or ridicule usually attracted by the belief especially from those to whom it appears foolish or unreasonable. Nevertheless, from the fundamental root of its practice, a belief is a course demanding not only life but soul. It excludes our whims and fancy. It expects an unalloyed loyalty in crisis as in peace, in poverty as in death. It calls for some of our most powerful sympathies and demands our undivided allegiance even before those to whom we are bound by strongest and most consecrated ties.

So far, in the Florence' saga, a moment of trial had come. In other words, a time to prove the type and stuff of her belief had dawned. Such a time will always come in the life of every pilgrim. However, questions that readily crop up the reader's mind are, did she win or give up? Did she stand or bend at last? But that her belief fell away or stood upright will be too early a matter to be preoccupied with at the moment. Instead, let us swing back to the story line and find out.

The officer in charge of Block 6 had abandoned Florence to starve for days thinking that the cravings of hunger and thirst for water would compel the woman of irrevocable decision to throw in the wet towel. That made Florence to spend good six days in that dark smelling cell, grotesque for human habitation. Dreams and nightmares had served her the worst in their stock. To talk about thoughts coming to her that moment is non-issue. Because on their own, they had ballooned beyond her control. No doubt, they had also 'helped' Florence to become older for her age.

It may be useful to disclose that a loss was always incurred by this regime whenever a Christian died in those cells. This, in the first place, means that the officer's chance of making a Beast's disciple out of such a person was averted and such a one has clean escaped receiving the mark of doom. In the second place, it means the concerned person has obviously escaped the inhuman treatment and torture of the heartless agents of the Antichrist.

If there was any conceivable reason for which Florence should go ahead and receive the Antichrist's '666' Mark, at least with the unflagging courage already displayed by Mercy, her convert, right before that brutal fire, such a reason, you will agree, should have loosed its grip on her or be said to have disappeared in the puff of smoke. To the greatest surprise of the officer, at the end of the day, Florence was yet swollen of assurance that Jesus was her Saviour, and neither was her determination to die in Christ relaxed from whipping her along. Little wonder the officer was perplexed as to just what he should do not to tell the same story of loss about Florence the way it was with Mercy.

Being controlled by the spirit of the Antichrist, the officer had to come up with an idea, of course, it was their time, you know. But what was the idea of the fiend? This officer went ahead to connive with the Raiding Unit to fetch either Dave Pauli, Florence' husband or Nathan their child to the camp. Given the house address and description, the raiders headed for Florence' residence. On getting there, the Beast's officers realized that Dave had received the mark on his forehead just the previous night and had started displaying those callous attributes of a doomed soul hauling most nauseating abuses on God. Not only that, he had also begun to threaten Nathan to trust in the Beast. The boy in turn was busy replying his father in the following words "Daddy, but my mum said Jesus is Lord and not the Antichrist."

"No, your mum is wrong," has been Dave's reply all the while. If you clap your eyes on this primary-three boy, you will almost shed blood after your tear gland has run out of tears. He appeared sickly and palely, with eyes beaten far into their sockets by grinding hunger. In other words, he was a metaphorical walking corpse. Yet, his confession remained homogenous of his mother's. He just went ahead asserting what his mother had been able to drive into his mind with utter disdain for the consequence.

By what the child upheld, coupled with his utter indifference to his father's blasphemy, the raiders, on getting there did judge well that Nathan must be precious to his mother. That is why they snatched him away from home to the Old June Camp. On getting to the camp, they gave him food and took proper care of him.

On the third day, having been neatly dressed up, he was informed that he was going to meet his mum. What news! Also prior to that fateful morning, Florence herself had received a notice that her attention was needed in the registration office.

Meanwhile, an hour to the time Florence was brought forth, a pot of about 6ft wide and 7ft deep, full of hot red oil, heated by fire to boil and stew with angry steam had been made ready for her decision. That if Florence insisted that Jesus was her Lord, Nathan, her bosom child should be thrown inside the cauldron of boiling oil. But if she had a rethink and received the mark, she should be released with her child.

So, at 10.00am, Florence was matched down to the registration office where her child was waiting to meet her. Before coming down, Florence herself had been given food after many days of starvation. All these measures were aimed at winning her mind for the

Antichrist's mark. At last, Florence came. Nathan had hardly sighted her mother at a distance when he jumped up to go and meet her. Tears blurred Florence' sight when she saw how hunger had gnawed the handsome boy to something that passed for a skeleton. The boy on the other hand was busy asking, 'Mum, where have you been. Are you sick that you're hospitalized here?' He was a child, he did not understand. That is why his mum's answer had remained, 'Nathan, don't worry, you'll understand by and by.' Eventually, they both settled down in that big office waiting for the next line of action. Not long, one huge red-eyed man 'stumbled' in, who, without greeting, enquired,

"Are you Florence, woman?"

"Yes."

"Stand up and follow me with your child."

Florence and Nathan stood up and followed him. Not long, they came to a building still in that camp. It was the size of a warehouse. It was in that building the pot of hot oil was awaiting Florence and her child. The man that escorted them down handed them to two other men who appeared much terrible and remote in their facial outlook than he.

"Are you Florence Pauli?" One of the fierce looking men demanded.

"Yes sir."

"Do you still want to stick to your belief and lose your child? Or are you ready to change by taking the mark and both of you go home free?"

"Officer please, I can't take the mark, my faith is precious. This boy is likewise dear to me."

"You're to choose, woman! Choose between your child and '666'. Receiving it regains you your freedom; rejecting it offers your child the cauldron of hot boiling oil."

"Officer I beg, as for this mark, I can't take…"

"Wait, people don't waste time here. What did you say? You mean this innocent child should die?"

"Christians don't die but sleep…"

"Shut up! You'll see now whether they sleep or die…"

With annoyance, Nathan was violently retrieved from her and thrown inside the cauldron of hot boiling oil. Immediately, the angry oil began to sizzle: *shuinng… shuinng* as Nathan fried away like a meat. Florence groaned; she wailed but the boy had passed on.

The officer's anger grew hotter in him and ordered that Florence also be fried like her child. Immediately, she was thrown inside the cauldron of boiling oil. She cried aloud as she fell inside it. She troubled the oil. At last she gave up the struggle; she gave up the ghost and disappeared to settle below the steaming oil. Florence died a hot death in deed, but she never dropped her conviction nor recanted her faith.

How terrible to be a Great Tribulation witness. It is gruesome to be part of those that will tell the story.

27 - THE NEXT CASUALTY

So far, by governance and policy, Coveland had proved itself up to merit that she was one of the sophisticated countries of the time. A heterogeneous state, she had really played host to virtually all the ethnic nationalities. This is why to meet her multilingual challenge, when the reign of terror began, the Antichrist had to employ the service of those Coveland citizens who understood some foreign languages. Those employed were to work in print and electronic media to relay to users of non official languages information released in the official language by the Antichrist. As such, native speakers in Coveland coastal regions who made use of only dialects would not be left out while foreigners could have programmes, plans and policies of the Antichrist communicated directly to them in their mother tongues.

This is what led to Chief Hassan, father of the *raptured* San Hassan, enrolling with the Beast's administration having being an Arabic teacher for years. After his employment, he was posted to State Security Department of the Antichrist in Coveland. He too had '666'Mark. Of course, that was the major criterion for any employment at that time. People said it was fond of him to display so conspicuously the '666' logo on his face cap when going to office. This goes a long way, at least, to tell someone how unashamed he was of his office. The major assignment of his unit was to go about and locate homes and offices of Christians who were against the mark. After locating their residence, they were to bring the address to the Raiding Unit to work upon.

In one of those days when Hassan came around to pay a condolence visit to Mrs. Frank whose husband had just died (because Mr. Frank's health was impaired by the chaotic 'weather' of that time leading eventually to death by cardio-vascular disease), he saw some tracts around. Prior to this time, out of compassion for the lost and now being their Pastor (Meadow County Pastor), Ray Fred had sent some tracts to Frank's residence so that those neighbours and sympathizers who probably had not taken the mark could read those tracts and be saved. One of the tracts was entitled 'The Antichrist and You'. Another was 'Take 666, Sign Your Doom'. Chief Hassan took notice of those tracts where they laid on the centre table and took a copy to get the address of the distributing church. Unfortunately, no church address was put. He wondered which church could have had such rude effrontery to have printed such offensive tracts at that sensitive time. Hassan made up his mind, of course, for the mandate he had received as a State Security Officer, to embark on meticulous investigation on the church concerned. Not long, he discovered that the same pastor he knew very well was the culprit. Because faint heart never wins fair lady, Chief Hassan had to exercise a great deal of patience to locate Ray's whereabouts since Daily Showers Interdenominational he used to know him with no longer existed. Information soon reached him that Ray Fred was holding one prayer meeting secretly somewhere at Meadow County. With this, Chief Hassan began an advanced secret investigation. Some weeks after, Ray was arrested with others as Roseline Abdullah, Mrs. Frank and a few others. While Ray was kept in the police net, all other members in Diaspora were being daily witch hunted all about

Ray was first put in a cell that looked so much like a Dickensian slum, in the way it was festooned by giant bugs, huge mosquitoes and made so 'rich' in putrefying odour. Series of allegation of serious consequences were levelled against him. He was called a rebel for distributing such offensive tracts. He was labelled a coup plotter for ever gathering people together to think about a religion that stood in opposition to the incumbent ruler. Accused of economic sabotage, Ray was also said to have been collecting money from those attending Meadow County meeting.

However, that evil genius never put anybody to death without first placing him on trial, at least, for the benefit of doubt. That is why having been stripped of his garment and left only with just a pair of knickers, Ray was brought out of cell to the open place in the Old June Prison to defend himself after seven days of severe hunger. Two officers of highly eloquent tongues were arraigned against him. Questions blasted from them like bomb as all prisoners and prison workers watched afar the tragic scenario.

"Pastor Ray, do you agree that you're a rebel?"

"No, I don't because I never carried arms nor gathered soldiers to seize the power that be."

Paa...paa, Ray was served with two solid but ignoble slaps on both cheeks by one of the officers. The reason for the slaps they did not explain. However, from the look of things, it was to correct Ray not to defend himself with such assertion any longer.

"Ray, do I hear you say again that you're not an enemy of the State after rejecting '666' and encouraging others to do away with it?"

"I never see it that way in as much as ours is a secular State where citizens have freedom of choice, even of religion."

"So, the Meadow County group was a human-rights fighter and you are an advocate of liberty? Answer me!"

"Not so. That's not the purpose."

"What's the purpose? The initiative not yours?"

"No, it's divine."

"You're a bloody liar. Why didn't the Divine receive you to heaven when He withdrew others years ago? I said you have a hidden agenda you've not disclosed. You are a conspirator, a notorious enemy of the State. We aren't fools. I can mention four or five people among those who had no portfolio or office like you do who still went away with your Jesus that day. You wicked rebel and coup plotter, where were you then? Or were you not the Pastor of the church of 'come as you are'. Now, you're calling yourself an end-time pastor and you're gathering people underground in order to topple the government of the Beast."

"Please I went astray the time Christ came, but..."

"K-e-ep sh-u-t, you went away or what did you say?" ridiculing him.

"Ast-ray," Ray replied in tears.

"If all these allegations are false, prove to us by collecting 666 Mark now!"

"No, never!"

"Then where is that real evidence that you're not a rebel? If really you want freedom, quickly collect the mark. If not, go ahead and declare your stand, and waste no time, friend!"

"Officers, please a banner is raised before me. It must be kept unfurled though the conflict is tense, though the battle is fierce. There is no going back here. Jesus remains my Lord and Christ my Saviour. To Him I owe total allegiance."

"Thank you 'Mr. Pastor'. We too are loyal to our master. You will serve as a deterrent to other rebel Christians who would not obey the power that be and authority of the State. In the name of the Beast, Pastor Ray Fred should be tied to a motor and be shamefully dragged around the camp in the presence of all and sundry."

Immediately this statement went out of the lips of the commanding officer, in a high speed, a motorcade sped out from somewhere that looked like a motor plant in that camp. The motor appeared like the Ford model of 1930s, with '666' as registration number. Its driver was hefty, dressed in Antichrist Police Uniform with a red helmet for head, black face guard like those of Mobile Police coupled with a remote countenance. The vehicle was painted black like the Police Black Maria. The siren light was in the dark blue. However, it never blared: hoi...hoi...hoi...the way police vans do. Rather, it went ahead to sing the Antichrist's anthem. Everything about the scene was frightening as some thick and palpable cloud of cruelty overshadowed the premises. Anyone who is chicken-hearted will not watch for long.

With a rope, Pastor Ray's hands were immediately tied to the back of the automobile. At the command of the officer in charge, this wagon began to race round the big compound that was more or less like a football field in its spherical shape, dragging Ray Fred along in a speed that stirred up dust. It was his legs that first began to peel. Other Christians watching the gory sight were perplexed, tapping fingers and crying: *eh...pah eh...pah* afar. Soon, his ankle bones had been grounded off. Soon, sharp stones had chopped up his knee bones. In excruciating pain, Pastor Ray cried aloud bleeding and bleeding profusely. After twenty minutes or thereabouts, his bowel had started busting out while his tongue was hanging out. In another ten minutes later, other parts had gone with soil, remaining only Ray's head and arms. Pastor Ray dared death courageously and went away to meet his Lord just like that, dying the most ignoble death. The gruesome exercise having not pacified the anger of the commanding officer, he instructed that Ray's head and arms be thrown into the cauldron of boiling oil. Immediately, his instruction was carried out.

Unhindered, those remaining parts of Ray fried away *shuinng...shuinng* just like that as soon as they landed inside the boiling oil.

28 - THE LAST ACTED

Observation, among other things, has shown that often times anywhere called housing estate, to an extent, has some environmental characteristics similar to that of a GRA, where, as you know, serenity or, if you like, quietness, is common place. Residents of places like those mentioned above often prefer flowers in their surroundings for aesthetic purposes, car park within the compound, bell at the main entrance and an eye-piece lens in the door through which to peep and see that stranger who stays outside busy knocking. All in the name of privacy or what do we call it? However, the opposite is the case in the public residences mostly in those congested areas of the town. There, all you have as a daily experience begins with the raucous radio noise in the morning and harsh sound system in the afternoon. If not an ear-splitting horn of a heavy truck in the evening, expect the rat-a-tat of a passing rickety auto. In effect, as this contrast has unavoidably divided our society into two, so had it done to Coveland.

To remind you, Roseline Abdullah was a housing estate lady, born and bred in a quiet, serene and scenic environment. This had informed certain of her behaviour. However, since her parents left the world in the Rapture of the saints, Rose had been attending Pastor Ray's Meadow County underground meeting following her restoration to faith through her brother's letter from Springfield. She was one of those in attendance when the Antichrist's Policemen invaded the underground to round up Pastor Ray and his people. She had since been locked up in one of the Old June's Cells.

The arrest of Meadow County Christians involved only twelve people, others escaped. Out of those twelve, Ray was the first to die. Later, three were asked to deny Christ by taking the mark of the Beast or otherwise hold live electric cable carrying high voltage from a 200kv generator set. Those involved preferred Jesus to the Antichrist and had to die by electrocution. On holding the cable, they got burnt up to ashes right on the spot. Another four, including Mrs. Frank, were tied to stake after refusing to take the mark. There were these six hungry tigers withdrawn from Coveland zoo, and had been starved for days. For want of food, they had roared and roared, and gone berserk, crazy or bananas, if you like. On Saturday morning of this ugly incident, those fierce-looking tigers were let loose. Having been trained to treat anybody tied to the stake as a robber, these wanton destroyers were hardly loosed when they had rushed out galloping like an Antelope in pain of a double barrel bullet, when they saw these Christians at distance. Remember, it was six against four. What do you call that? Survival of the fittest or of the fastest? Come and see the struggle. They angrily rushed at them. Their clothes were torn to rags within twenty seconds. With carnivorous voracity, they tore them to pieces eating their flesh, licking their blood and masticating their bones. It was a bloody Saturday and a gory sight.

The remaining four people never knew the type of death that awaited them. That is why continually their prayer was 'Lord, help us to endure the hour of tribulation.' Roseline Abdullah was one of the four people that remained from those arrested at Meadow County underground. When Roseline was arrested she had about twenty tracts on her which eventually followed her to the prison. Just after the brutal death of Pastor Ray, Roseline felt the brutality employed in killing Ray might make some Christians in the Old June Camp drop their conviction. As such, she felt she should secretly slot in those tracts into their cells to serve as a means of boosting their morale after reading it. For days, serious and sustained efforts were made without fruits.

The price was costly, of course. If Roseline was caught, she might suffer a much terrible death than that of Ray. Notwithstanding, the more cruel and torturous the officers' exercise was, the more active and unrelenting Roseline's zeal was to execute the last duty with deeper commitment. She knew it was only by sacrifice she could realize her goal in that terrible prison camp where ordinary air breathed smelt of the Antichrist. After the most careful study of the time, especially the time prison officers would go to mess hall for meal or to their base to sleep, Roseline, whose cell's door was not difficult to open, quietly went through the corridor and gently threw those tracts inside the cells of her fellow Christian prisoners. What a dangerous attempt! A risky mission indeed! The secret plan was safely executed at last. Obviously, that was the correct thing to say because nobody saw her, not even the Christians in the cells concerned. But by next morning when light had beamed into the prison and the inmates had seen the tracts, they wondered, taking it for granted that an angel had visited them overnight. Besides, reading a title as 'Take 666, Sign your Doom' appeared the strongest warning nobody else could give at such a time except God. That is why the threatening and intimidation of the Antichrist began to crack, losing its grips. Immediately, the number of those recanting their faith fell sharply. Saints began to endure their sufferings and death. Even those about whom plans had been concluded to be matched to '666' centre within the camp the following morning to receive the mark for no readiness to die for Christ just changed their minds overnight, deciding to hold on to the cross be it in form of stake, be it in form of boiling oil!

The change that came in overnight in the response of these Christian inmates soon brought some headache to the murderous Beast regime. A lot of investigations were carried out. No meaningful outcome attended their efforts until someone after six days or thereabouts discovered one of the tracts which one prisoner had carelessly displayed. Immediately, officers went round the cells and inquired whether they had all received the paper. When it was discovered that everybody had read it, madness seized the authority; it threatened; it cried foul; it spat brimstone. However, Roseline's goal had been achieved. While questions and queries mixed together, shouting rose and fell everywhere in the camp, and terms as 'betrayal', 'mutiny', 'disloyalty' and 'fifth columnist' were used freely as Antichrist's officers kept asking the questions: 'Who's that rogue that did this?' At last, when no tangible solution emerged, the remaining three men from Meadow County were taken for scapegoats. Untried, they were thrown into the cauldron of boiling oil. These 'blind' officers had resolved in their minds that a female prisoner as Roseline could never have engaged such a risky adventure. Would you not call this a yet another *'ignorantia a judicis est. calamitas innocentes,'* that is, the 'ignorance of the judge is the calamity of the innocent'?

Immediately after the death of the three brothers, Roseline repeated the act twice before she was caught on the third attempt. After catching her, she was taken to Rebel Collaborators' Cell. She was the eighteenth person to ever go there and, of course, the first female. In the day anybody from Rebel Collaborators' Cell was to be executed, just that person would be killed. Period. All other prisoners must watch the scene from A to Z. They must join Beast officers to sing aloud the Antichrist's Anthem on their feet before the ordeal commenced.

On the day of her execution, Roseline was brought out into the open place. Her demeanour was not sad. Her countenance expressed determination. In spite the hunger, her face was beaming with hope and joy unspeakable. Around the place where she was tied were two big drums closed. After all the questioning of the officer handling her case with constant affirmative reply that 'Jesus is Lord and my Saviour!' of Roseline, the drums were opened. Immediately, two big frightening pythons crawled out. Come and hear how clatter of screaming and thunderous shouting began to rumble at different quarters of the camp. There was nothing Roseline or anybody else could do. If Roseline decided to change her mind at that point, never would she be able to alter the verdict; because, already, the die had been cast. Neither oath nor sacrifice counted any longer. Rather than recanted, Roseline closed her eyes firmly and called: 'Jesus help m-e-e-e-e'. The smaller of the two python moved near her and curled around her. E-e-sh! Imagine her feeling. For long, this snake stretched her beyond limit. About twenty minutes later, it had broken her spinal cord. She fell and died, blood oozing out of her nostril, mouth and ears. After this, the second python began to swallow her up from her legs little by little until only her shoulders and head remained outside. At this point, it appeared Rose remains could no more go in. That was how the two pythons began to crawl away into a place that looked like pig pen where they lived. It only took some days; Roseline's head soon got spoilt and fell off. However, the real Roseline had joined the great company of myriad saints at the Celestial City.

After Roseline, such a sight was a regular occurrence in the Old June Camp in Coveland. Yet the history was not over or the curtain was drawn over the nation amidst the tension of the Great Tribulation and imperial decrees, in a world vexed by terror, horror and cruelty of gruesome murder with unrestrained scourge of catastrophe happening in rapid succession. Impoverishment did ravage unchecked; anarchy was let loose on earth and Antichrist's killing rose unabated. Lingering agonies of death are obvious in the on-going seven-year Great Tribulation, and there are more eerie days to come, days of turned-down sympathy and refused pleas for mercy.

Still lying ahead are woes and unspeakable troubles as the on-going 7-year Great Tribulation is brought to a close with the Battle of Armageddon. In other words, at the end of the on-going Tribulation, Christ will come back physically (the period known as the Second Advent) with all the *raptured* saints to establish His one-thousand years of literal and peaceful government on earth. At his arrival, the Battle of Armageddon will take place (Rev.19:11-20) it will put an end to the insurrections of the Antichrist, the Beast and the false Prophet, while Satan himself is arrested and sent to the Bottomless Pit for the period of one thousand years to trouble the world no more (Rev. 20: 1-3). Then will the Millennial Reign of Christ begin which will last uninterruptedly for good 1000 years (Rev.20:1-7). Following the Millennial Reign is the Second Resurrection which involves only all the dead sinners of all ages beginning from the time of Adam (Rev.20: 5, 6, 12-15) to be given their final sentence right at the White Throne Judgment. The White Throne Judgement will be the most frightful, fierce and dreadful trial anyone can be summoned. However, it will remain a fair and just delivery of the most incorruptible Judge of the universe (Rev.20:11-15). Next shall emerge the New Heaven and New Earth (Rev.21) which shall descend from our God when the endless days of rest and righteousness will begin for the redeemed in a demon-free universe of only the holy people and blood-washed saints; in the kingdom void of all rebellion, revolt and uprising of heartless men; in a world devoid of corrupt practices of nations, of kings, of lords and over lords, with pain and poverty forever gone. Amen, so let it be! And there let our portion be.

"Surely I come quickly, Amen. Even so, come, Lord Jesus." Rev. 22:20

Printed in July 2023
by Rotomail Italia S.p.A., Vignate (MI) - Italy